USA TODAY BESTSELLING AUTHOR

Dale Mayer

TERKEL'S TEAM SERIES
GAGE'S GOAL

BOOK 03

GAGE'S GOAL: TERKEL'S TEAM, BOOK 3
Dale Mayer
Valley Publishing Ltd.

ISBN-13: 978-1-773365-15-2
Print Edition

Books in This Series:

About This Book

Welcome to a brand-new series from *USA Today* best-selling author Dale Mayer, where dark-ops SEALs have special senses and skills, needed to solve intrigue, betrayal, and ... murder. A series with all the elements you've come to love, plus so much more, ... including psychics!

Gage hadn't told the rest of his team, but he'd planned to meet up with Lorelei after their team disbanded. A little one-on-one time was needed to see if all the sparks they'd felt over the last few years were the real thing. He'd deliberately avoided getting involved with anyone he worked with, so this seemed like the perfect opportunity. Until all the team is decimated ...

Lorelei was in Manchester, hoping to run into Gage, but after a car accident that sent her to hospital with an injured leg, she had no idea what had happened to the others, until Terk contacted her. Once he realized what had befallen her, he figured out that her accident was likely no accident and probably the same potential annihilation that his team had experienced. Terk coaxes Lorelei to live in their temporary new headquarters, where she finds out Gage hadn't contacted her by choice but because he couldn't.

Now on the mend, Gage is determined to keep her safe, only that's much easier said than done, as the attacks turn on her and just ... won't ... stop.

Sign up to be notified of all Dale's releases here!
https://smarturl.it/DaleNews

PROLOGUE

G AGE HILLMAN OPENED his eyes. He was pretty damn sure that Terk had done something to knock him out. Gage was just afraid that he may have been knocked out for a few weeks. He slowly sat up, shifted his gaze, and realized that he felt damn good. He got up, went to the bathroom, and, when he walked out to the main room, there was a sudden silence, as everybody turned to look at him.

Then Tasha hopped to her feet, from where she'd been sitting with Damon, and came running. Gage opened his arms and held her gently. "Am I right to assume that old doofus finally broke down and did the right thing?"

She chuckled. "Well, it might have taken a little bit of convincing," she teased, then returned to Damon.

Damon rolled his eyes at that. "Hardly." He got up, walked over to Gage, and asked, "How are you feeling?"

"Like I've been hit by a concrete truck, then dumped into a river and shaken off a little bit," he replied. "How do I look?"

"About like that." Damon grinned.

Gage walked forward, rolling his shoulders front and back. "Actually I don't feel all that bad. Just kind of stiff. How long have I been out?"

"A couple days," said another woman, sitting off to the side.

He looked at her, his brain trying to pull out the correct name. "Sophia, was it?"

"Yes, I am Sophia." She stood and shook his hand. "I'm with Wade."

Gage looked at Wade, who shrugged.

"You remember the night that we were attacked about a year ago? I was out with her that night," Wade explained. "I was supposed to meet her the next night for dinner, and, of course, I didn't show up."

"Of course not," Gage stated, in complete understanding. "We don't like to bring danger to other people. Especially those we care about."

"Well, in my case," Sophia replied, "I've been working with Levi's team for the last year on a few jobs here and there. The minute I found this guy again, I didn't let go."

"That bad, *huh*?"

"Well, that good." She smiled a cheeky grin. "I get why he walked, but he doesn't get that opportunity again."

At that, Gage burst out laughing. "Sounds great," he replied, happy to be conscious and to feel better. "Now that I'm alive, do we have any news? An update at least?"

"Not a whole lot of news yet," Terkel replied. He shifted, stood, stretched, and walked over to Gage, studying his friend.

"Thanks," Gage said sincerely to Terk. "I don't think I would have survived that alone."

"No, I don't think you would have either. It's been touch-and-go for all of us," Terk murmured.

"So no new intel?"

"Not yet." Just then a message came to Terk's phone. Terk pulled it out and read it. "Anybody know a Lorelei?"

"We all do. Lorelei worked in the government," Gage

stated.

At that, Terk froze, turned, and looked at him. "Your Lorelei?"

"She's hardly mine," he replied, "but she's my contact, yes. We all know her but didn't see her much, as she's stateside."

"Well, I think that same Lorelei has a message." He read it to the team. "*You are in danger, all of you. Go under and stay safe.*"

"Isn't that a little late for a warning?"

"Or it's a new warning," Sophia suggested.

"And that's possible too." Gage nodded, as his finger hovered over the message. "Let me send her a reply message."

"Wait. Does she even know you're alive?" Terk asked him.

"No, I don't know that she does." He frowned. "And I guess we don't want her to know."

"Most people know I'm alive, and that's partly why we're still being hunted," Terk explained.

"Of course they are," Gage agreed. "You always were the hardest one to kill."

"Damn right," Terk murmured. He sent Lorelei a message. **Can you help?** When his phone rang, he was given a series of numbers to dial on the other end. Eyebrows raised, he quickly punched them in.

When he was connected, a woman answered, "This is a secure line."

"Lorelei?"

"Yes," she answered, her voice heavy. "Oh my God, Terkel, I'm so sorry."

"Do you have any idea what happened?" he asked.

"I don't know all the details, no," she replied, "but I

overheard something about your team being wiped out."

"Depends what *wiped out* means," Terk stated.

"I only just heard, and that's why I'm calling you."

"Yeah, why's that?" he asked, putting his cell on Speakerphone.

"Have you"—she stopped—"have you heard from Gage?"

"Ah," he said, looking over at Gage. "Why?"

"Because I really don't want to think that he's dead," she replied. "But now that I heard that something happened to your team, I'm really worried about him."

"And with good reason," Terk said. "Do you know what happened to us?"

"No, not specifics, I don't. They were just talking about a major attack. And I don't understand why," she explained. "You were supposed to be disbanded. I was hoping to hear from him, once he was done there. 'Cause I know he's always been against any personal relationship, while he worked for that division."

"That's because of the danger involved." Although Terk had come to believe—for himself, as well as the members of his team—that finding the right partner, the one who could meld in with the rest of them, was a plus, not a minus. Was a good grounding mechanism for these guys, who carried extra-big loads of stress and expectations and levels of success on their shoulders. And having exceptional women on board, who could be mates and part of the team too, bringing their own special skills? *Wow.* Terk shook his head that he and the guys had not seen this particular element of their lives in a more open manner.

"I get that. I really do," she replied anxiously. "Please tell me. Have you heard from him?"

"And what difference would it make now?" Terk asked, frowning.

"I'm in Manchester," she said abruptly.

At that, his warning signals went up. "You're in Manchester?"

Gage instinctively took a step forward.

"Yes," she confirmed. "I came over here, hoping to talk to him, as soon as you guys were done. I flew in that Friday. And then I found out."

Silence. Shocked, Gage and Terkel stared at each other.

She rushed to speak again. "And I know you won't believe this," she added, "but I was hit by a car that next morning. I've just gotten out of the hospital myself."

Everybody froze.

"Seriously?"

"Yeah," she confirmed in a small voice. "I don't know if it's connected."

"I would say it's a little too close in time and place *not* to be connected," he replied. "I need to meet with you. Where do you suggest?"

"I don't know." She hesitated. "I've got a safe line 'cause I'm the one who used to arrange them," she noted, "but I don't know about a safe place. I've checked into a hotel, so maybe here."

"That works." Terk looked at Gage, who was motionless in front of him. Terk quickly wrote down her address. "We're on our way." Then he hung up and faced Gage. "What do you think?"

"Let's go." Gage walked to the door. "That son of a bitch. It's not just us who were attacked. Sounds like everybody who had anything to do with us too."

"Yeah, and we've lost our government access and support as well," Terk noted. "This is bigger than just us. But it still doesn't change the fact that we're the only ones, really the only ones, who are in any position to fix this."

Gage nodded. "Damn good thing I'm feeling better, *huh*?"

"Yeah, damn good thing," Terkel agreed, with a wry eye roll. "Now you want to stay healthy, please? The more of you guys who go down, the less energy I have for myself."

"That's not true," Gage argued, whacking him on the shoulder. "It's just you're too stuffy and don't want to take it from anybody else."

Terkel laughed. "Whatever," he replied. "Let's go. Do you think she'll be happy to see you?"

"Damn, I hope so," he stated. "It was good to hear her voice."

"And what about the worry in her voice?"

"Well, she's right. I was hoping to see her afterward," he noted. "We hadn't discussed anything formally. She did have holidays coming up so ... but I would wait a day or two."

Terkel nodded. "Apparently you guys all had plans."

"What were yours?" Gage asked his friend.

"Go to Texas to visit my brother. Now, if and whenever I get safely from here," he added, "there's a woman I need to meet."

"A woman?" Gage asked, turning and looking at him. Terk explained, and Gage's jaw dropped. "Seriously? A stranger carrying your child?" He frowned. "You know that she could be behind all this."

"No. She's suffered at the hands of these assholes herself. She's also still in a coma, or at least was two days ago, when I last talked to Ice."

"Jesus, man, that sucks." Gage couldn't believe the

lengths these people had gone to. "Especially when I know children are an issue for you."

"I know, but, until we get a little more information, I'm not bringing her into any more danger by going there myself."

"And why her? What did she do to attract attention?"

He shrugged. "At the moment we have no idea. And, of course, we've been a little busy."

"But you know that's something to follow," Gage stated.

Terk nodded, grabbed his jacket, and stared at the rest of the team.

Tasha turned to Sophia. "We will do a deeper dive into that."

"Yeah, you go meet Lorelei," Sophia said. "You guys solve that problem, and we'll get to work here."

"Done," Terkel noted, and together the two men left.

As Gage walked out the door, casting one last glance back at the small group, he had to wonder if just the three of them were left from the original team. What the hell had happened, and how would they get to the bottom of this? Then he looked at Terkel, striding forward, and Gage realized the *hows* didn't matter. Because Gage could count on one guarantee. And that was that Terkel was determined to solve this. And he'd solve it in such a way that everybody else would pay the price for having crossed them.

And Gage was good with that.

CHAPTER 1

G AGE, WITH TERK at his side, moved slowly through the downtown Manchester area, heading toward the hotel where Lorelei waited. Gage was one of the searchers of the group, somebody who could send out advanced energy, looking for anything dangerous. But now, with his energy damaged, almost fractured, he could only send out probes ten to fifteen feet in front of him. He murmured to Terk, "I am close to zero help to you in this shape."

"If you're referring to the leg, don't worry about it." Terk shrugged. "We're all physically injured to a certain extent. And, as far as the energy goes, anything you can offer is still more than we could expect from anybody else."

"Sure, but it's one thing to send out a probe and to realize something's out there. It's another thing completely to send out a probe and to realize I can't even get it out a few feet."

"What is the distance now?" Terk asked him curiously, as they crossed the road, keeping an eye out around them to see if they were being followed.

"I'd say twelve feet—maybe fifteen if I push it."

"Versus?"

"A couple hundred," he noted, with a broken laugh.

"And can you feel anything within that limited space when you send out the probe?"

"Not so far." Gage shook his head. "So I don't even know if it's working effectively at that."

"Well, it's working," Terk pointed out. "We just don't know if it's a power issue. You can always take some from me or from someone around you, if you need to."

"I've tried," he admitted, "and I'm not taking anything from you. You're already half supporting the rest of the team."

"And you also, to a certain extent," he added, "but I haven't been giving you full power because of that."

"Don't think I haven't noticed," Gage said sharply. "Do you think I like the fact that I can't seem to function on my own without you?"

"You will eventually. You just need some time," he stated, comfortably.

Gage groaned. "You know how I feel about not keeping up on my own."

"So, heal faster then," Terk replied, with a teasing smile.

"Yeah, if only it were that easy." He tilted his head. "Right before the attack on the team, I had just sent out probes into our operations to see what they were up to."

"*Hmm.*" Terk seemed interested.

Gage looked over at Terk. "I wonder if that had something to do with them shutting us down."

"I was just wondering what the trigger was."

Gage nodded.

"Like what brought this on and what was happening that made them think we needed to be shut down at that particular point in time. If you were starting to access other people's mental space with your abilities," Terk guessed, "maybe they found out somehow, and that was one of the things they decided made us too dangerous."

"I don't know," Gage replied. "I never thought of it that way."

"And we don't know that *that* is what prompted whoever to shut us down," Terk stated. "I'm just always contemplating the reason why, trying to understand."

"It would be nice to confirm though, wouldn't it?"

"Yes, it sure would. Damon and Wade and I were wondering if they had a technology-based version of our team, ready and available to operate, and, as such, we were no longer needed. In fact, we would be more dangerous than any IT because they couldn't control us."

"That's also a good reason to test any software on us, while shutting us down," Gage agreed. "Wade did fill me in a little bit on that."

"Good," Terk noted. "It's been a pretty confusing time, with everybody slowly regaining abilities and, so far, still not quite up to full form. We're hampered and really shorthanded."

"Yeah, it feels like we're hampered all right." Gage exploded with laughter. "That is definitely the understatement of all time."

"Hey," Terk reminded him, "we're alive, and those of us who are functioning to some degree at least are doing whatever we can."

"I get that," Gage conceded. "It just sucks that what we can do doesn't appear to be very much. Not very much at all."

"Well, it's still a damn sight more than we were able to do last week," Terk noted. "And, at that point in time, I'll remind you, you were still out cold."

"I know. And you had guards on us too, didn't you?"

"I tried," he admitted. "And I started to get worried that

maybe the guards would talk, so I ended up changing them out on a regular basis."

Gage shook his head. "I really do owe you my life, man."

"You don't owe me jack shit," Terk replied in a harsh voice. "Just help me deal with this, so we can at least have a life afterward, without looking over our shoulders forever."

"Do you think that'll ever be possible?"

Terk didn't reply.

Curious to see and speak with Lorelei, they walked through the lobby and straight to the elevators. They deliberately kept their faces away from the cameras, and they were both wearing hats and overcoats. A little bit much for the weather but at least they were dealing with some rain outside. Inside the elevator, they relaxed ever-so-slightly, just not as much as they would have liked to.

Some things were instinctive, and others were impacted because things were still not quite up to snuff. A camera was in the elevator as well, so they kept their backs to it, until they stepped out on the right floor.

Once they made it to the room, the door opened easily under the twist of Terk's hand on the knob. They stepped inside, Lorelei standing behind the door, her eyes huge. She held a finger to her lips, then held up a small device.

Making a soundless exclamation, Gage took it from her and swept it around the room. And, sure enough, in the lampstand on the far side of the bed was a bug. He took it out and dropped it in a glass of water and then did another sweep. When it came back negative, he nodded. "Okay, it's clear."

"Thank God." Lorelei then walked over to Gage and picked up his hands and stared at him. "My God, it's good to see you." She asked him, "Are you okay?"

He gave her a lopsided grin, then tugged her into his arms. "Well, I'm really glad you're asking, but I'm about 50 percent okay."

"Well, sorry to say it, but I wouldn't have guessed even that much, based on that slight limp and the way you look right now."

He burst out laughing. "Well, there goes my ego. And here I thought I was doing so well."

She shook her head. "Like your ego needs any stroking." She snorted in disgust. Then she turned and looked at Terk, walking over toward him. "You don't look so great either, you know?"

His gaze was strong and steady, as he smiled at her. "We love you too," he replied gently.

She flashed him a look and shook her head. "It's been really tough."

"Tell us what happened with your accident."

"I don't even know what to say." She shrugged, turned. "I was walking across the street to my home, and a car came out of nowhere and hit me. I think the only reason I'm still alive," she guessed, "is that, in the last split second, I had an instant reflex. I jumped back, so it just caught my hip and leg." She pointed to her leg, still in a walking brace.

Immediately Gage frowned and asked, "Is it broken?"

"No, it isn't." She shook her head. "Thankfully it's just severely bruised and twisted. We thought this would be the easiest way to keep the alignment, while it slowly strengthened again. It's one of those braces that you put on daily. I had it in my apartment from a prior injury my sister had, so I thought, why not? It does feel better too."

Gage bent down and took a look at the leg. "The bruising is pretty bad for ten days later though."

"Hey, it looks wonderful now," she joked.

He stood, frowning. "When you said it came out of nowhere—"

"Yeah," she added, "suddenly the vehicle was just there. I mean, maybe I was daydreaming or something. Maybe I just didn't see it. I don't know." She wrapped her arms around her chest. "But honestly it was freaky the way it happened."

He nodded quietly. "Any thought that it might have been deliberate?"

"Not until I heard about what happened to you guys," she noted. "Then, yeah, I've had lots of thoughts about it since then."

"Any conclusions?" Terk asked.

"Well, I think an asshole out there is hunting me. So it would be awfully nice to find him and to ask him those kinds of questions."

"Yep, I hear you there," Terk muttered. "Give me the details again. Where were you? Which corner was it? What time of day? Where else had you been?"

Calmly she went over it all again, providing as much detail as she could. "I was at home and decided I was a little short on groceries. So I walked up to the bakery just around the corner." She pointed in that direction. "On my way back, I was crossing the road." She walked over to the window, slowly limping her way there, then pointed to the corner. "It was that corner there."

"So, you were almost home then," Terk confirmed.

She nodded. "Almost, yes. And then all hell broke loose, and my peace and safety were taken from me."

"I'm sorry," Terk said. "It sounds very much like you were targeted, just as we were."

"And that's what I'm afraid of," she stated. "I just don't

know why they would have targeted me though."

"I don't know either," Terk agreed. "I don't know why we were targeted, for that matter." He faced her. "Have you been back to work?"

"No, I was given medical leave," she replied, "and there's no sign that my job is in jeopardy."

"Has your access been reduced at all?"

"No, actually my boss asked me to do up some reports from here at home on my own time. Whenever I feel like it of course," she noted, with an eye roll. "So my access hasn't been limited."

"Well, that's a blessing at least," both men said.

She shrugged. "Not really. It's only a blessing if somebody is not tracking me while I'm at it." She pointed at the lamp where the bug had been.

"That is quite possible as well," Terk agreed. "We also lost somebody else in the department. Bob."

She nodded. "I heard about that, but I didn't think it was related. I heard he had a heart attack."

"A convenient heart attack, I'm sure," Gage noted.

"It just never occurred to me, until you guys were injured," she replied.

"Wait. This corner right here?" Gage asked.

She nodded. "My apartment is on the other corner over there." She pointed down the street.

"Why did you choose a hotel so close to home?"

"Partly hoping it might deceive them. And partly because I didn't know where else to go, and at least I knew about this place," she replied. "Plus, I haven't been able to walk very far."

Terk nodded.

"Chances are good that you shouldn't be staying here

though," Gage stated.

"I don't have anywhere else to go," she admitted.

"I understand," he answered. "We'll have to find you a place and keep you safe."

"I'd like to stay wherever you guys are," she told them.

"Nope," Gage said instantly.

She glared at him. "Why not? If this is related to you, I'm already in danger."

"Quite true," he noted, "but we can't look after you the way you need to be looked after."

"Nobody else is around to look after me," she clarified. "And, if the government is after me, which I hope to God it's not," she added, "I can't fight it anyway."

"I would hope it's not the government, but we don't know that," Gage murmured.

"I know. I know," she agreed. "And I shouldn't have said that, but, I mean, you must have suspicions about it."

"Obviously," Gage stated, "and you're right to worry. It's just that we don't have answers yet."

"What do you know?" she asked, sounding frustrated.

Gage frowned, looked to Terk, and then slowly filled her in on some of it.

"So some of the team is okay then," she stated quietly, "but not all."

Gage shook his head. "No, not all, and we're not letting anybody know if anybody is okay or not."

"Facial recognition would have picked up the two of you," she pointed out, "if anybody was looking anyway."

"Yes, that's true," Gage confirmed, "but we must move around some, just to keep our intel going. And, since everybody is still not at full strength, we're in danger of being taken down just because of our weaknesses. Thus we do some surveillance, which requires the risk of getting around."

"The disguises help of course." She looked at them both again. "I almost didn't recognize you when you walked in."

"Well, it's us," Gage stated quietly. "Now the problem is, who is after you, why are they after you, and does it have anything to do with us?"

"I can't see how it would be a separate issue," she replied, "but I guess it's possible."

"Is there anybody else in your world who would like to see you dead?"

She looked at Gage quietly and nodded. "Yeah, my ex. We separated over two years ago, and he's pissed at how the divorce came out."

"And is that something he would kill you over?"

"If he thought it would give him the inheritance, yes."

"What inheritance?"

"My family has money," she explained, "and I recently came into several million dollars."

"But if you two are already divorced, how does he figure he would get access to that?" Gage asked, tilting his head and studying her.

"Because I got the money before we were divorced."

He winced at that. "So doesn't that mean it depends on how the judge viewed the details of the case?"

"Yes," she agreed, "though it all happened in the same time frame, so it's definitely been an ugly scenario. However, the judge ruled in my favor, so it's my money, and my ex is definitely not in my will. So I don't know whether it could have been pettiness or maybe, you know, his final answer. Like it would serve me right. Or who knows? Maybe he has another plan in mind to get the money."

"Children?" Terk asked her.

She shook her head. "No, but I do have guardianship over my sister, who also received a large sum of money."

"Guardianship?"

She slowly nodded her head. "Yes, my sister is under full medical care in a home," she explained. "She was hurt in a bad car accident, when she was eight years old, and she's not been capable of living on her own ever since."

"So she also has the same amount of money?"

"More actually," she noted, "and she'll need it to see to her care for the rest of her life."

"So, as her guardian, you dispense that money as you see fit?"

"Correct." She nodded. "Which, in my world, means, looking after my sister. But, in my ex's world, maybe not. Honestly he wanted her brought home and a nurse hired to look after her."

"So, to some people, that would seem a better option than a more institutional setting," Terk added carefully, looking at her. "Does she know you?"

She shook her head. "Honestly there's very little movement, period. She's more or less catatonic. She eats when she's told to eat, with help of course. She's bathed and dressed and looked after on a regular basis. But it's not a great life for her. Yet having her at home won't help her. She's comfortable in the surroundings she knows. Every time I've taken her on a day-trip outing or something to enliven the boredom of her life, she experienced full-on panic attacks. So moving her would not be a good scenario."

"And why did your husband think it would be better?"

"Not better, *cheaper*," she noted bluntly. "He figured we could hire a nurse for fifty grand a year or whatever, versus the half a million her care currently costs. Of course that includes security as well."

"Ah," he nodded, "so it's more about money for him then."

"Apparently it was always about the money," she replied quietly. "Unfortunately I was a fool and didn't recognize it. But I was also in love and thought that, you know, he felt the same way."

"That's not always the way it works, is it?"

"No, it isn't," she agreed. "If he did this, I would have absolutely no problem making sure he spent the rest of his life in jail." She shrugged. "But I don't have any way to confirm it was him or not."

"You didn't recognize the vehicle?" Gage asked.

"No, it was a dark sedan, smoked windows," she described. "Honestly, my thought at the time, when it went flying by, was an official government vehicle, but I didn't really have the chance to think."

"And, if you did think *government*, did you happen to recognize the driver?"

She shook her head immediately. "I didn't see anything. It all happened so fast, and then I was in the air. Once I hit the pavement, I was unconscious and was taken away in an ambulance. And maybe that's why I'm still alive," she added. "People were around. Otherwise the vehicle might have come back around the block and finished the job."

"So you definitely feel it was deliberate."

She nodded. "Yes, it felt deliberate, and I've never doubted that. It felt like he waited until I got to the sidewalk and just sped up toward me. I didn't really hear it until, all of a sudden, he was there … and *bam*."

"SO WHY DID the hospital let you out so early?" Gage asked her studying her face intently.

Lorelei winced. "They didn't let me out. I discharged myself." They both stared at her. "I didn't feel safe there," she stated simply. "What if he found me again?"

"Right. Of course that's another worry," Gage noted reluctantly.

She nodded, grimacing. "The thing is, when I was in the hospital, I felt like somebody was checking in on me one day. I opened my eyes to find a stranger there. I started screaming, and he disappeared, and a nurse flew into my room. She told me that it was all okay and that I'd just woken up after a bad accident."

"Did you tell her that somebody had been there?" he asked.

"I did, but she told me that nobody was around and that I was imagining it."

"Great," Gage muttered, "and, after that, it probably went down on your chart that you were imagining boogey-men everywhere."

"Exactly," she murmured. "When I said I didn't feel safe in the hospital, and I didn't want to stay because I didn't like their lack of security, I'm sure they thought I was paranoid or delusional. I already knew the scope of how that works because of my sister, and I refused to stay long enough for them to label me and to send me for psychiatric treatment."

"Good call," Terk noted, "except it's left us without any lead to follow."

"Exactly," she agreed, "but it has also left me without anywhere to go. I called you because I'm here, and this is where the accident happened, and I was hoping you might have some information. I really wasn't planning on dying at this stage of my life."

"That won't happen," Gage declared immediately.

She snorted and just looked at him. "You look like shit too," she stated, "so I can't imagine that you'll be a whole lot of help in stopping it."

"You might be surprised," he replied, his gaze hard.

She raised her hands, palms up. "Look. I'm not trying to insult you. Honestly, that's definitely not what I'm trying to do, but I don't know where to turn anymore," she admitted. "If I can't come wherever you guys are, what am I supposed to do? I can't go home, and I can't spend the rest of my life, sitting in a hotel, where I could be discovered at any moment by whoever bugged this place."

"What about the bug? Any ideas?" Terk asked her, pointing to the thing in the glass.

She frowned, shook her head. "I don't know where it came from," she replied reluctantly. "Again I was hoping you would have more answers."

"I don't have any." Gage quietly studied her. "What's interesting is that you felt the need to check for a bug."

"Yeah." She nodded, with a shrug. "I've been working for the government long enough to become obsessed with security."

"When would it have been put in?"

"Either before I got here," she noted, "or when I went to the rooftop to soak my leg in the hot tub."

"And when was that?" Gage asked.

"This morning. When I came back, the room felt different."

"And again, good instincts," Gage murmured, then walked over and gave her a gentle hug. "I'm glad you survived whatever this was."

"I'm glad you survived too," she replied, misty-eyed.

"The question is, what will we do about staying alive?"

Terk looked at her. "Have you got much gear with you?"

She shook her head. "No, I just grabbed a few things from my apartment. I don't have much here at all. Why?"

"Good, less to pack," he replied.

Lorelei looked at Terk, hope in her heart. "And where would I be going?"

He looked over at Gage, who was shaking his head.

"Don't do it," Gage told Terk. "You know as well as I do that it's too dangerous."

"It's dangerous for her here too," Terk added. "We can't just leave her like this, and we have no one to guard her. They've already tracked her down, so they know where she's staying. The next step is to annihilate her, but they haven't. They brought in a bug."

"And now they also know that we're here or that somebody came and that the bug has been found and removed," Gage noted, as a reminder. "Therefore, they know that somebody else has tracked her down and that she's being watched by more than just them."

"So, the answer is," Terk stated, studying his friend carefully, "she comes back with us. Then, using her abilities and her log-ins, she can help us to track down whoever's doing this."

"Done," she said instantly, glaring at Gage. "You don't get to say anything about it."

"I'm just trying to keep you safe," he protested.

"There is no keeping me safe now. Don't you understand that?"

At that Gage fell silent; then he nodded reluctantly. "I guess she would be safer with us than us trying to keep her safe here," he admitted.

"My thoughts exactly," Terk replied quietly.

CHAPTER 2

P ACKED UP AND in the vehicle, Lorelei winced at the
pain that moving so quickly had caused. She refused to
allow herself even the tiniest squeak over it though, not
wanting to give Terk and Gage a reason to change their
minds and to keep her from joining them. She sat ever-so-
still as they moved.

"You can relax, you know?" Gage noted from the front
seat. She looked at him but with a haunted gaze and asked,
"What if they watched us load up?"

"We'll lose them now," Gage said quietly.

"Have you guys been attacked since you've come back to
whatever level of normality you have?"

"Too many times," Terk replied quietly.

She gasped. "That's not good."

"We didn't say it was safe to be with us, but we determined—along with you—that it would be the best of what
are all bad options."

She nodded. "I'm still coming. You can't change that,
Gage."

"I'd like to. I'd really like to know that you'll be safe."

"So would I," she replied bluntly, "but apparently that's
not an option in our world anymore."

"Well, it will be again one day," Terk noted.

She shook her head. "This is all just nuts. I don't know

why they did this. Whoever it is."

"And that's what we'll have to find out," Terk murmured. "Did anything at work happen before the accident? Anything that was odd or different? Did you get your clearances changed or anything?"

She thought about it. "I've been racking my brains over what might have happened or not have happened," she noted, "and it's been really tough to find anything. But there was a change of command, and I ended up moved."

"What do you mean, *moved*?"

She shrugged. "Under a different supervisor," she explained. "I wasn't really happy about it, and they knew it, but I don't think anybody really cares."

"Of course not," Gage noted. "It's the government. You do the job, and you aren't supposed to become the job or to get emotionally attached in any way."

"Of course not." She shrugged. "But how do I work with all these people and not get emotionally attached? It's hard."

"Of course it is," Gage added sympathetically. "So, considering that, when you said you didn't like your new boss, what did you really mean?"

"I felt like I was being watched all the time. And I know new bosses are bad for that anyway because they want to know that you can do the job and can be relied on and trusted. But this was different, and it just seemed like, any time I was on the phone, he was suddenly there, as if I couldn't have a private phone call or talk with a friend or something. A couple times I got calls about my sister, saying she was having a bad day, asking if I could come by and see her later that day. When I got off the phone, he was asking me what the call was all about. I was upset because it was already a privacy issue, and I didn't really want to deal with him, but he made it very clear that private phone calls weren't allowed."

"Sounds like an asshole right there," Gage muttered.

"Yeah, but we can't just blame that. I've worked with plenty of assholes before," she noted.

He laughed. "True enough. We can't avoid them, but it sure would be nice if we could."

She smiled at him. "Then I had the accident, and I didn't really have much to do with him anyway, as I'm working online."

"Well, who asked you to keep working, now that you're at home?"

"My old boss. When I did get a chance to talk to him about the shuffles at work, he said he had no idea what had happened or why. He did say he would try to get me back into his department because he really couldn't afford to do without me," she explained. "I have to admit that made me feel better because I don't want to go back if it means working for this other guy."

"And who's to say that you will go back at all or that any of the people you've been working with will even be there when you return?" Terk asked. "It's like that sometimes."

"I don't like that idea," she murmured. "I'd like to have a little more trust, a little more optimism in my job, a little bit more joy."

"More joy would be good for all of us," Gage murmured gently.

She looked around and asked, "Where are we?" There was absolutely no panic inside her, just curiosity.

"Still in Manchester," Terk replied.

She knew these men, and she especially knew Gage.

Not that anybody else knew that they had a connection, and she couldn't really say what they were because, when they had first met a year ago, they'd hit it off to the extent that they didn't want to separate. But he had gone overseas again, and, since then, they hadn't seen each other face-to-face for a long time. And when a friendship is distanced like that, it didn't seem as if they could develop into a further relationship.

But she had known in the back of her mind that someday it would happen; it just was wrong timing for them. Then they had both been attacked, and now she had no idea what was happening. She didn't know if he had somebody else in his life or what else was going on in his world.

But, for the moment, she felt safe and protected, and, in a world gone crazy, a little bit of stability was on her horizon, and she was damn glad to have it. She closed her eyes and relaxed in the safety of their company, letting the motion of the vehicle lull her to sleep. She heard them talking quietly in the front seat but tuned it out, confident that, if anything needed her attention, they would wake her up.

When she opened her eyes again, her passenger door was open, Gage nudging her awake. "Are we here already?" she asked, rubbing her eyes.

"Yes," he replied gently. Looking down at her leg, he asked, "Can you walk?"

"I walked into the elevator," she noted, "so why wouldn't I walk now?"

"Because I know you're hurt worse than you're letting on," he murmured, "and you're being stubborn about it."

She gave him a look, batted her eyes, and said, "What? You mean, being stubborn is just a male thing?"

"Nope, not at all." He grinned, as he helped her down.

She felt the shock of the landing on the concrete all the way up her spine and immediately knew the color was disappearing from her face.

"Like I said ..." And, with that, he gently put an arm under her shoulders. "Come on. Let's get you inside."

They were at a weird warehouse-looking facility. "Where are we anyway?" she murmured, looking around.

"Well, it's home. It's not very much to look at, and not a whole lot of it is set up for us, so it'll be tight quarters," he explained, "but several of us are here."

"Good," she replied. "That sounds about right. At least the others will be here to help you."

"Maybe, but they've also got their own issues," he murmured.

"Of course they do." Lorelei nodded. "Everybody was hurt, weren't they?"

"Terk got off the easiest," Gage added. "Though, ever since, he's been putting himself at risk, trying to keep the rest of us alive."

"But then that's Terk, isn't it?" she noted, equally quietly. "That man has never been very good at letting go."

Gage laughed. "Especially not for those he cares about."

"I'm surprised his brother isn't here too."

"He is actually. Do you know about Merk's or Levi's group?"

"Just a little bit. I remember talking to Terk once and him saying that he and his brother were close, but that their paths were ever-so-slightly different."

"I think that goes for all siblings, doesn't it?"

"Maybe." She shrugged. "I don't know." Once inside she took a deep breath. "Do we have much farther to walk?"

"Nope," he stated, "but, if you want, I can carry you this

last bit."

"No, that won't be good," she replied. "I want to go in there not under my own steam."

He nodded. "I get it, but nobody will think worse of you."

"Maybe not," she stated. "I'm just getting very, very tired." And, with that, he helped her limp forward, until suddenly they were in a large room. She stopped, looked around at the people staring at her. It took a few moments for her to get her bearings, and then, with a weak smile, she lifted a hand. "Well, Damon, this isn't exactly how I thought we'd meet again." Immediately she was engulfed in a gentle hug.

"Hey Lorelei," he said. "I hate to say it, but you look like shit." His arms were quickly replaced by Wade's.

"You guys are going to make me cry."

"That's okay too." Wade nodded.

She gazed around the room to the two women. Lorelei immediately smiled at Tasha. "Gosh, I haven't seen you in a very long time."

Tasha walked over and gave her a gentle kiss on the cheek. "I'm so sorry to hear what happened to you," she said.

Lorelei nodded. "Let's just say it's been a shit couple of weeks." She looked at the other woman and frowned. The other woman frowned at her.

"So, I'm not sure if both of you frowning means you guys know each other or what," Tasha admitted.

"She looks familiar," Lorelei said bluntly, "but I can't put a name to the face."

"I'm Sophia."

"Ah, the accent," Lorelei noted. "Now I remember. You've been at several of the computer conferences I've been to." She frowned again, concentrating. "Weren't you there with part of Levi's group?"

"Do you know Levi?"

"Yeah, he's been involved in a couple jobs for the government," she nodded, "and his name has come through a time or two."

"So see? You know just enough to be dangerous," Terk stated. "I wonder if it wasn't the government attacking us after all." At his call for attention, and, with Lorelei sitting in a chair with her leg up, Terk filled in the rest of the team on what had happened at their meeting with Lorelei. When he was done, he looked back at Lorelei. "So, either you have a private party after you, or your case is another part of our nasty puzzle as well."

"Because of the timing," she noted, "I wouldn't be at all surprised if it was the same thing."

"But because a ton of money is involved with you personally," Gage added, "it could be either ... or both."

"I know," she muttered.

"By the way, did you ever get to see your sister?"

"That day I did," she confirmed. "And unfortunately, by the time I got there, she was not cognizant."

"And she doesn't even recognize you?" Sophia asked, sorrow evident on her face.

"No, she doesn't typically, but sometimes being around me makes her calmer."

"Of course," Sophia agreed. "She might not recognize you by sight, but, maybe on an energy level, she does."

"Well, that's what I was hoping," Lorelei noted. "Realizing a little bit of what you guys do here with your energy work, I've been researching it, wondering if I could help ease her pain somehow when she's having those really tough days," she murmured. "But unfortunately I haven't gotten very far."

"It is an avenue you should pursue though," Terk agreed, surprising her. He looked at her, then smiled and added, "There really is an awful lot we can do on an energy level, particularly if you're coming from the heart."

"It will always come from heart with me," she stated firmly.

"Good enough." He looked around at the rest of the room. "So, we now have another person involved, another case involved, and she's also injured. I'm hoping we have enough room here to keep expanding, but living on top of each other will be a bit of a challenge."

"Not a challenge at all," Sophia argued. "We're all adults. We're all in trouble, and we know that, if we don't help each other, we'll all be in bigger trouble."

"You're right about that," Terk agreed.

"So it's really not an issue, and we still have several other bedrooms—like another four or five, isn't it?" Sophia asked, turning to look at Tasha.

"Overall it is a pretty big place," Tasha noted. "However, we're contained to just a part of this warehouse. This common area and the private rooms. The smaller closed-off areas aren't necessarily bedrooms, but they are rooms, some with bathrooms included. Some of the other bathrooms are accessed down the hall."

"I'm happy to go wherever you put me," Lorelei replied. "I just really didn't want to stay at the hotel anymore."

"That brings up another point," Terk addressed the team. "There was a bug in her room."

At that, Gage fished it from his pocket and handed it to Tasha. "You want to see if you can find some information on that?"

She stared at it in shock. "Seriously? They bugged her room? That just sucks."

"Yeah, it does," Lorelei agreed quietly. "It's really hard to trust when you realize that, the one time you left your room, somebody went inside and planted a bug to see who you're talking to." With that, she looked at Gage. "Any chance I can go lie down?" she asked, desperate to keep the tremor from her voice, but knew she had failed when Gage frowned at her.

"I knew we should have put you in a room right away," Gage snapped. "You've got to stay off that leg." He picked her up in his arms against her protest, then turned to Tasha and asked, "Do you care where?"

Tasha laughed. "I'm not the house mother, and I'm definitely not the house chatelaine." She shook her head, smiling at her quips. "Find a room that works for you and use it. Like I said, it's a mixed bag. Go take a look and find her one with a bathroom attached, if you can. Feel free to move anything in the way. It should be pretty easy to see which rooms we're already using."

"Okay, we'll go take a look," Gage replied, and, still carrying her, he left the main room.

Lorelei whispered to him, "Is everybody staying here?"

"Yeah, everyone who has gotten well enough to join us again, and it's safe here for us at the moment," he noted. "We have security set up, and nobody can get in or out without us knowing. So we're staying here at the moment, while we track this all down."

"Good." She sighed, laying her head against his shoulder. "I can't say I'm unhappy to hear that at all."

"Of course not," he murmured, "but it doesn't mean

that we can get smug about security."

"No." Lorelei yawned. "That would be the worst thing. That's when they sneak up behind you, and, *pow*, they've got you before you even know it."

"Which is exactly how they took out our two admins, Wilson and Mera," he noted quietly. "He was killed, shot in his sleep. They tried that with Mera and shot her as she slept, but she survived. She insisted on hiding on her own, and later they followed up and took her down. They tried the same with Tasha, but she heard him coming and made it look like she was sleeping, then hid. Thankfully she came in, when Damon found her. It was just Damon and Terk then, and neither were in that great of shape."

Lorelei stared up at him. "I didn't even think to ask about Mera and Wilson. My God," she said. "What the hell's going on here?"

"Which is why I didn't necessarily want you to come here," Gage explained, his tone grim. "This is not all sunshine and roses, and we don't have a fraction of the answers we need."

She stared at the firm jaw above her, then stroked it gently. "Maybe not," she whispered, "but I know one thing. If there are any answers to be found, you guys will find them."

And, with that, he gave a clipped nod. He walked over to a doorway, and she reached out and turned the doorknob for him. Inside was a large room with a bed and a bathroom attached.

"This is perfect," she said.

He laid her gently atop the bed. "I'll go grab your bags." Then he turned and walked out, but, when he went to shut the door, she called out.

"Don't, ... please."

He stopped and looked at her. "Don't what?"

"Don't, … uh, … don't shut the door, please."

He frowned, then looked at her for a long moment and nodded. "I can leave it open. But enough people are here, working and living, that you'll probably want to close it at some point."

"That's fine for later." She nodded. "I'll want a lot of things in life, and I'll get them, one step at a time."

And, with a nod, he left.

GAGE WALKED OUT to the main room, exhaling loudly, as he put his hands on his hips, and he studied the group. "Is it okay that she's here?" he asked bluntly.

Immediately the women turned to face him.

"Absolutely," Tasha replied.

"Of course," Sophia chimed in.

He couldn't detect any falseness in their answers, so he turned to look at the others. It was Damon and Wade that he was worried about.

"Of course it's fine," Damon noted. "We don't have any place better equipped, and obviously the two of you have a relationship."

"Well, I don't know about a *relationship*," Gage corrected quietly, "but I sure don't want to see her get hurt."

"She's already hurt," Wade reminded him.

"Yeah, and what we don't know is whether that was part of what happened to us or it was something entirely separate. It would sure be nice to figure that out."

"We've already run down the ex," Tasha noted, "and pulled the records on her sister."

"Why her sister?" he asked, looking over at her.

"Just in case anything was funky about her long-ago accident," she said, with a raised eyebrow.

He nodded and accepted the stack of papers she had printed for him. "Thanks, I'll read through this, but can you give us the short version verbally? What did you find?" he asked, flipping through the documents.

"The sister was badly injured in a car accident at eight years old, caused by a drunk driver, who lived another four years in prison and later was killed by another inmate."

"So, can't blame that on the ex," Gage noted.

"No, not him, and he didn't seem to have any family. Lorelei's ex has not remarried. He's currently living in Paris and isn't doing very well financially these days. When they were together, not only was she making a healthy wage but he also had a government job at the same time and was doing well. Between them, they had a comfortable standard of living, but, once they divorced, he lost that. Then she inherited a pile of money that he felt should have been his."

"So, does he look like a killer?"

"No, but anybody who loses that kind of money has the potential to kill," Terk noted quietly.

"I know," Gage nodded. "I remember her talking about the divorce."

"You've known her that long?" Damon asked.

Gage nodded. "Yeah, we've been friendly for years." He shrugged. "I knew that she was getting divorced, and that it was ugly, and I just stayed out of the way."

"Good thinking," Terk noted.

"Maybe not. Maybe, if this guy knew somebody else was in her life, he wouldn't have gone after her."

"Well, her ex has been going after her in multiple ways

but mostly legal," Tasha explained. "And I don't see that somebody who is playing this kind of a legal game would also go after her physically. This has been going on for a couple years."

"Unless …" Damon turned to join the conversation from the other side of the main room, looking at them. "Unless it was evident that he had no other recourse, though it still seems like a bit of a stretch."

"And what about the bug?" Wade asked. "Are we really thinking that bug was related to him?"

"It's a standard-issue government bug," Tasha noted.

"If there was ever a tip-off that this is likely a government operation, it would be that, wouldn't it?" Sophia asked.

"Yeah, but, on the other hand, these bugs aren't that hard to get a hold of, and who knows what they were looking for from Lorelei. Maybe they were suspicious that she was working for somebody else and were using this in the hopes of finding out. I don't know," Tasha added. "And I'm still tracking down her log-ins."

"Or you can just ask Lorelei, and she can give them to you." Gage looked at her.

Tasha waved her hand dismissively. "Sophia tracked down the ex almost immediately and started running down his recent addresses, financials, and property ownership. Same for the sister. So, I switched to hunting through the government databases, and I'm looking to see if anybody else is checking in on her emails."

"If she was working part-time for the government still, even while on sick leave," Gage noted, "there shouldn't be anybody in there."

"Yeah, I hear you," Tasha said, bending to look at her screen. "But, if that were the case, I don't think this person would have logged in recently."

"What? You can tell the time when somebody has logged into your emails?" Gage asked.

"When it comes to the government, you can always tell," Tasha stated, "because everything is hidden or available for tracking. Somebody was in there on the day of her accident."

"And is there anything in her emails that's suspicious?"

Tasha looked over at him, and her lips twitched. "Does that mean you're giving me permission to scan through them?"

"Absolutely," Gage replied. "I trust her, but, if anything's to be found, let's find it now. And it doesn't mean that it's even necessarily something that's suspicious. It's just got to be enough to trigger the government. And, honest to God, that sometimes doesn't take much at all."

She nodded. "I'll get back to you on what I find, if anything looks out of place."

He waited, but she didn't seem to be getting anything too quickly, so Gage walked over to where Terk was sitting and asked him, "Are you sure we did the right thing?"

"No," Terk admitted quietly, "but our options are pretty limited, and, if her accident's in any way related to our team's nightmare, you and I both know Lorelei needs to be here. And, even if it's not, we don't have a way to protect her anywhere else."

"I know," Gage agreed, "and I don't want her alone, but, at the same time, I don't really want her to get any more mixed up with this than she already is."

"Already too late for that," Terk noted. "Way too late."

Gage groaned because Terk was right; it just wasn't what Gage wanted to hear. "I need to get answers," he murmured, then threw down the papers in disgust. "And, as much as I know we have some theories about what's happened up until now, I'm definitely still a little shaky on some of the details." At that, Tasha handed Gage a binder. "What the hell is this?" he asked, looking at Tasha.

"Case notes," she replied bluntly. "It's the only way we'll keep track of everything and bring each person up to speed as they come on board."

"This just covers the two of you, you and Sophia," he noted in astonishment, as he quickly flipped through it.

She nodded. "And this is just about Wade and Damon," she added, as she handed over another binder. "Terk will tell you about his own case in his own time."

At that, Gage stopped and turned to his friend, an eyebrow raised. Terk stared at him, but the grim cast to his face told Gage more than he wanted to know. "Dear God," Gage said. "What the hell is going on?" In a low voice, Terk explained about the woman at Levi and Ice's compound.

"So you know her name is Celia, but that's it?"

"We don't have a match for her fingerprints. We don't have DNA matches. We don't have squat," Terk replied. "We really don't know anything about her yet."

"Well, that's pretty damn frustrating. So how do you know it's your child?"

Terk stared at his friend, his gaze relentless.

"Oh, energy, I presume," Gage noted, and Terk nodded slowly.

"Yes," Terk agreed. "I was out after my previous injury and for a pretty long time. We were wondering if the harvesting happened during the time I was unconscious."

"I hope not for your sake," Gage stated. "That would be pretty rough."

"It would, indeed," Terk agreed.

"Regardless, I'm really sorry. It sounds terrible." Gage frowned.

"It is." Terk nodded. "I'm also worried about her. I don't know how she's involved in any of this. I don't know if she's an innocent victim or what. I don't know any of it." He shrugged. "For now it's a wait-and-see thing."

Gage was stunned. It was unbelievable to think that some woman who Terk had never met was pregnant with his child.

"And to think that they could have done something like that while you were out cold. Talk about invasive." He shook his head, feeling violated for his friend.

"And unfortunately, although she's alive and supposedly physically well, she is not awake, and she may not even know she's pregnant," Terk added.

"But it hasn't been all that long, has it?" Gage asked.

He shook his head. "No, and Ice is giving me daily updates. But I don't have any more of that part of the story that I can fill you in on."

"Okay." Gage asked, "And the drones?"

"Yes, we've been gathering a lot of information on that. We've got the blueprints and the supposed builder, young William Poma. He's one of the dead. We have two separate IT guys—brothers, Randall and Rodney Godwin—who were killed in two separate homes, after they became redundant, plus several others are dead as well," Terk added. "So there's definitely action but just not enough intel."

"Not enough but it's progress. Anything new on the drones?"

"Actually, yes," Tasha noted. "As soon as Sophia returns, we'll fill you in on it."

With that, Gage had to be satisfied. He walked over and

put on a pot of coffee, then asked, "What about food? We're starting to get a lot of us here."

"Somebody will have to go on a food run," Tasha noted. "A few sandwich fixings are in the fridge, if you want something right now though."

He opened up the fridge and realized that's about all there was. "Somebody needs to go for food today. I guess we should have grabbed it while we were out."

"Yeah, we probably should have," Terk admitted. Just then he got a message. He lifted his phone and read the text. "My brother wants to meet."

"Perfect," Gage replied. "I'll go with you, and we'll grab food while we're at it."

Terk nodded, standing. "Can you go now?"

"Yeah. Let me just make a sandwich, and I'll bring it along. Want one?"

"No thanks. Are you doing okay? You're probably about due for a rest."

"I'll be okay, just need to put some fuel in the tank. I'll get a break when we return." With that, Gage pulled out some sliced cheese and meat, slapped it between two slabs of bread coated with mayonnaise and butter, then nodded. "I'm good to go." Grabbing his jacket and his sandwich, he walked out the door.

Once inside the truck, he turned to Terk. "Is there anything that nobody is telling me yet?"

"Nope." Terk shook his head. "A lot of pieces to the pie you probably aren't up to snuff on, and you'll have to spend some time going over those binders Tasha gave you," Terk noted. "It's important. We do have names and faces and dates, but, so far, nobody is left alive."

"You guys have had to kill them all?" he asked, turning

to look at his friend.

"No. Not us. Whoever is doing this isn't leaving any witnesses behind."

Gage nodded at that. "Not the first time we've seen the bad guys killing off their own," he muttered.

"Nope, absolutely not," Terk agreed.

As they drove, Gage asked, "Where are we meeting Merk?"

"Outside, at a park."

"Interesting," Gage muttered. "Is that safe?"

"Nothing is safe. Would you rather be picked off outside or pinned in a corner inside?" Terk murmured. "As for me, I'll go with Merk's gut on this one."

By the time they made it there, the sandwich had worked its way into Gage's stomach, and at least he felt like he wouldn't die of starvation anymore. But they definitely needed to pick up a huge load of groceries from somewhere. As he hopped out, he enjoyed seeing the twin brothers greet each other. They looked so damn much alike that it was uncanny. He walked over and smiled at Merk. "Nice to meet you."

"Likewise." The two men shook hands.

"Looks like life has improved a bit in your corner over the last few days," Merk said to Gage. "You're awake and on your feet at least."

"That's true. Today's been crazy. We picked up a friend of mine who works for the government and was recently run down by a car. We think it's potentially related."

Merk's eyebrows shot up. "Seriously?"

"Yeah, we're just not sure yet. We're tracking down everything to do with her world right now. Her leg is pretty banged up, and we've got her back at the compound, with the rest of us."

At that, Merk shook his head, then looked over at his brother. "Do you want to get some more security over there?" he asked. "I can bring over a couple more men for sure."

Terk frowned, thought about it. "I don't know, Merk." Terk paused. "I feel like we're better off if we stay small, but, as you know, we've had circumstances recently where it would have been helpful to have a few more people."

"You mean, more than me, huh?"

"Is that why we're meeting? Do you have to go back?"

"They're asking if I'm going back," Merk clarified, "but I'm gauging whether I need to go back or if I'm needed here more." Terk hesitated, and Merk nodded. "Good enough. I'm staying."

"I didn't even say anything," Terk protested.

"And you wouldn't have hesitated if you were sure what to say. Therefore, you need somebody, so it's a done deal. I figure on staying here for another week or so anyway."

"If you could, that would be good," Terk agreed. "I don't have full-time work, but we need people."

"This isn't about full-time work," Merk stated. "This is about my brother needing help."

Just as they stood here, smiling at each other, Gage picked up a glint on the hillside. "Duck." Instinctively he grabbed Terk and pulled him to the side. The shot missed all of them, but the three men bolted for safety to a group of trees off to the side. Not a sound was heard from up the hill.

Merk looked up at it, frowned, and whispered, "I'll go around and see if I can get him. We need to catch this asshole."

"You do that." Terk looked over at Gage. "You stay

here. I'll go in the other direction." With that, the two brothers split up and headed in opposite directions.

Gage was left standing by the trees, cursing, wondering what the hell had just happened. He checked his surroundings, using his own energy probes and his spidey sense. He confirmed the intruder's presence up above, but he had no idea who it was. It wasn't any energy signature that Gage recognized. He immediately sent out a message to Wade, asking if he recognized the signature of the shooter. Wade's voice was thin, but, whether that was due to his transmission or Gage's, Gage didn't know.

No came the answer. *It's a new entity.*

Great. Gage shut down that energy connection, as he headed toward the parking lot. He stayed close to the vehicles, keeping watch on the three other vehicles here, though one was a little farther away. That truck had the bed lifted and looked to be for somebody about nineteen years old, given the graffiti on the side. But Gage had seen vehicles like that used before because everybody would try a variety of ways to camouflage their true activities.

As he watched, a couple came down the park trail, laughing and joking. He wanted to tell them to hurry up and to get out of the way, but, of course, the pair didn't know anything was going on. They got into one of the cars and took off. That was good, for it left only two more, including the weird one.

Almost immediately somebody came from the opposite direction, walking their dogs. Gage leaned against Terk's truck and smiled, as they got into the other vehicle and left. That just left the graffiti one. Gage frowned as he studied it, wondering. There was no reason for the shooter to even be here.

When Gage heard a weird whispering in his head, he focused. Terk was trying to talk to him. "What's up?" Gage asked in a low voice.

The trouble with Terk was sometimes his transmissions came through clear, and sometimes they weren't. But the one word Gage did get was *trouble*. As in, somebody was in trouble. He straightened and looked in the direction Terk had gone. Gage didn't know what the hell the message was, but, if somebody was in trouble, he was on it.

He did a quick search around and then bolted for the woods in the direction Terk had disappeared. Almost immediately he saw two men up ahead. He slid into the shadows and approached through the woods. As he got close enough, he heard voices.

"I saw him, I tell you. I don't know where the hell he's gone, but he was right here."

"Look. I saw one of the guys on the far side," the other one said.

"Don't give me that shit. I didn't see anybody there at all. I'm telling you, the one guy I was trailing," he noted, "was here. I'm not an idiot, and I don't make up shit."

"I'm not saying you did," the other guy replied, using a pacifying tone, which just pissed off the other guy.

"He was here," he repeated.

"Well, he's not here now, so what the hell do you want me to do?" he asked. "If he was here, you lost him. If he wasn't here, you didn't, so whatever." The other guy shrugged. "We'll do a full search of the place, so it's not like they can leave. And somebody was standing by their vehicle, so keep an eye on that one."

"Hell, a lot of people have left already," he said, "and that guy was still hanging around there at the vehicles."

"Well, I don't know who he is, but something should already be happening."

"I don't know about that," he replied, "but I'll take off on this side and see what's there."

"Good enough. You do that."

And, with that, the one guy took off toward where Terk had been waiting.

Gage wondered if he should split off and take down that one, but instead he waited to see what the other guy would do.

Immediately the guy turned, pulled out his phone, and said, "This idiot you sent me lost him."

There was obvious outrage on the other end of the phone. Gage quietly snorted.

"Yeah, I'll take care of him," he replied.

With that, Gage swore and headed back down to the parking lot. They really needed somebody alive they could question, but if these guys kept killing their own people, there wouldn't be any chance of that. As Gage raced back toward their vehicle, he heard Terk in the back of his head, calling out again. Gage sent Terk a message, hoping he would get it, letting him know just what the hell was going on.

By the time Gage could see their vehicle, he found no sign of the other guy. He stopped in the nearby trees and turned and quietly looked around. *There.* Gage saw the guy on the far side, standing close against another copse of trees. Nearly hidden, just not quite good enough to do the job.

As Gage turned to look around one more time, he heard a single shot fired, and the guy crumpled to the ground. Swearing, Gage raced in the direction of the shooter and, by the time he got there, saw no sign of anyone around.

Feeling like he'd done nothing but run around and chase idiots, exhausting himself in the process, Gage waited until he heard Terk's message, telling him to stay where he was. Gage froze, knowing that Terk had abilities that most people didn't know about.

Meanwhile, as soon as Terk presented himself alongside the shooter, the guy wasn't even watching for enemies. When Terk made a warning sound, the shooter turned the rifle in his hand, trying to bring it to bear, but Terk hit him hard with his right fist to the jaw. The guy dropped.

At that, Gage stepped out, smiled at his friend. "Damn good thing you got him. He just killed the other guy."

"I was afraid that's what he was up to," Terk replied grimly. "They took a couple shots at Merk too."

"Is he hurt?"

"I don't know," Terk said. "He better not be. You want to go take a look? I'll keep this guy disarmed."

"On it." And Gage took off to find Merk. He hadn't gone but ten feet, when Merk stepped out of the bush, with blood on his forehead and a distinctly hard-ass attitude in his gaze.

"I would like just one minute with that asshole," he called out to his brother, as they both joined Terk.

"Not getting it," Terk muttered, "at least not until we're done with him."

"After that, he's mine," Merk snapped.

"Yep, have at him," Terk agreed. "We'll have to get rid of him somehow anyway."

At that, Merk gave a hard laugh. "These guys don't last long enough to be disposed of."

Gage nodded. "Man, they're cleaning them up pretty fast. I heard this one on the phone say something about the other guy had lost someone he was tracking, and apparently that's a failure they couldn't accept."

"They didn't have to kill him," Merk stated in disgust. "Even a bad guy's life should be worth a little more than that."

"It should be," Terk agreed, "but that's exactly what's been happening."

"We've got this one anyway, so it's all good." With that, Terk and Gage loaded their captive into their truck, then after a quick check into the other truck but finding it empty, they headed back to the warehouse. They'd have to grab the groceries on a different run.

CHAPTER 3

LORELEI WAS AWAKE. Tired, exhausted, sore, and not liking being alone. She slowly shifted, so that she sat on the end of the bed. She heard voices but not close enough to decipher who was there.

The memories came rushing back, as she realized where she was and how she'd come to be here. Finally she'd found Gage. At the same time, somebody had found them, according to him anyway. That didn't make her happy.

She hadn't spent all those years working for the CIA, without realizing a certain level of danger was associated with her job. She just hadn't expected it to come home to roost so personally.

She didn't know why she failed to foresee that, though obviously that was naïve of her. However, after she'd been hit by a vehicle, and then they'd found a bug in her hotel room, she had to wonder if it really was all connected. Until this was resolved, it seemed they just had no way to get good answers to a problem that didn't seem to end. Still, she had to trust that these guys knew what they were doing, so she didn't need to worry about it. At least she hoped so.

Her world was filled with too much mystery to even begin finding some answers. She slowly lay back down on the bed, wondering if she should just stay here and try to get more rest. Any movement killed her leg, not to mention her back.

Just when she thought that maybe she could snuggle back to sleep, an ever-so-gentle tap came on the partially shut door.

"Come in," she replied quietly.

The door opened, and Gage stuck his head around the corner. He smiled when he saw her, stepping inside. "Hey," he greeted her in a soft voice. "How are you feeling?"

"Like I got hit by a truck," she noted in an equally soft voice. "I was thinking about getting up, but all that movement just causes more pain than I really wanted to deal with."

He nodded. "How about a hot bath?"

Her eyes lit up with interest, as she contemplated the idea. "That might help," she admitted, "but it feels weird to have a nap and a bath in the daytime."

His lips twitched. "Well, in that case, you don't have to worry about that. It's seven o'clock already."

She stared at him. "Good Lord. I'll never sleep tonight."

"Oh, I bet you will," he noted, with a smile. As he walked closer to the bed, he sat down on the edge, his gaze studying her face, as it slowly flushed a beautiful pink.

"You don't have to make me feel like I'm such a mess."

His eyes widened. "Not what I was intending at all," he countered. "I was searching your expression, seeing how you really felt."

She winced. "Right, because everybody is a liar?"

"A lot of people aren't liars as much as they just don't want to tell the truth and to cause other people to worry about them," he corrected.

She nodded. "Well, that would be true in my case," she admitted. "I've also been on my own for quite a while, and

I'm just not used to telling people how I feel."

"Got it," he noted, with a quick head nod. "You don't have to do that with us though. You know that, right?"

She nodded. "I know you say that," she agreed, "but I still don't really know anybody here that well."

"And yet you recognized most of them," he murmured.

She looked over at him with a shrug. "My stomach is rumbling. Do you guys have a way to get food here?"

"We do," he replied, "and we resupplied our little make-shift pantry today."

"So, we're cooking, or how does that work?"

"At this point in time," he stated, "it's a combination of both, if you call reheating in a microwave as *cooking*. We picked up quite a bit of takeout—various Greek dishes. And we've got lots of bread and cheese, sliced meats for sandwiches, plus a few simple things to warm up. And then we'll put together another meal for tomorrow."

"You must be struggling with logistics," she noted.

"Yeah, since we don't have the usual avenues for help and for support that we're used to, it certainly makes it harder," he agreed, with a head nod. "But we are nothing if not resourceful, yet I feel bad that we can't provide something more comfortable for you. We're used to this and much worse, but we don't expect everybody else to be."

She frowned. "It shouldn't be about that."

"Nope, it shouldn't be, and it's not," he said cheerfully, "but it's amazing how something like a few little creature comforts can make things easier."

"I guess," she murmured. "I hadn't really thought of it."

"Luckily enough," he added, "you probably haven't been in a position where it was an issue. I think it's important that you understand what's going on and that it's temporary.

Because anything other than that just causes more stress."

She laughed. "I'm not so sure that anything will make this go away, except answers."

"Well, speaking of which—"

She looked at him expectantly. "Did you find out something?"

He nodded. "We did but not necessarily about your scenario."

She waved a hand at that. "Fill me in," she said, trying to shift in the bed.

"Why don't you get up?" he asked. "Let's go join the others, and we'll all discuss it and get you something to eat."

"Fine." She hesitated, then looked over at him. "Could you give me a hand getting up?" she asked, as she reached out a hand. He gently helped her to her feet. And, when he took a few steps aside, she frowned. "I wondered if you were limping before."

"Yeah, my leg is not quite back to normal yet," he replied.

"What happened to your leg?" she asked.

"Something to do with damaged nerves," he stated. "I've got a bit of a limp, and it doesn't quite pick up when I want it to."

"Is that likely to get better?"

"I hope so," he said cheerfully. "Doesn't really matter though. I've got to deal with it for now."

"I get it, but …"

He reached out, touched her gently under the chin, and raised her face to share a gaze with her. "You worry about you. I'm fine."

She snorted at that. "Oh, so you're allowed to lie, but I'm not."

At that, he burst into delighted laughter, and that's how they arrived in the main room. The others looked at him, but Gage just shrugged. "It's nothing,"

"Well, if it's something that you get to laugh at, it's obviously something," Sophia noted. "And I have to admit I'm jealous because there hasn't been a whole lot to laugh at lately."

Gage smiled, as he seated Lorelei at one end of the long table. "Lorelei's desperately in need of some sustenance." Immediately containers were passed her way. He served her a big plate, even though she protested.

"I said that I could do this on my own," she snapped. "I'm hardly an invalid, and I did get here under my own steam."

"You did, indeed," he agreed, without letting up at all.

She sighed. "There really is no help for it, is there?" she asked, looking to Tasha. "They just have to be these macho men."

"They have to be the protectors they are," Tasha stated, with a nod. "So it's easier to just let them do and be who it is they feel that they need to be."

"Hey, we're sitting right here, you know?" Wade stated, and the others joined in with affirmations.

When they were all seated and working their way through the food, Lorelei plowed into hers, not stopping until the first set of hunger pangs were appeased. Then she looked over at Gage. "So, what did you find out today?"

He launched into an explanation of their meeting with Merk. When he got to the shooting in the park and how their adversaries had taken out one of their own men, her jaw dropped. When he mentioned that they had brought their prisoner here, she immediately looked around the room.

"Where?"

"He's still unconscious," Terk replied, "and my brother is standing guard over him."

She looked at him in shock. "The prisoner's here?" she asked in a squeaking voice.

"Yep," Terk confirmed, "but he can't get at you."

She blinked several times, shook her head. "Wow, I have a little nap, and everything just pivots."

"Life is like that," Gage agreed, laughing. He handed her a container with more food, but she immediately shook her head.

"No, I'm good," she said. "This is a lot for me, as it is."

"Well, you need it to heal," he added, "so keep eating."

She rolled her eyes at him. "Seriously, I'm fine."

He assessed her plate, as if deciding how much she'd consumed and then shrugged. "Maybe. … You shoveled it in and moved around everything on your plate, so it's hard to know how much of it you ate."

"Thanks for keeping an eye on me, *Dad*," she teased. When he glared at her, she laughed. "Sorry, I didn't realize how much you hated that turn of phrase."

"Yeah, like everybody my age wants to be seen as a father," he noted. "Particularly a father figure."

"Well, that's never been your problem," she stated, with an eye roll, and then realized the others were watching their interplay with curiosity. She flushed, horrified, then glared at him and caught his grin. "Sorry, guys. We have a little bit of history between us that you probably don't know about."

"Well, we can see a connection is there certainly," Wade noted calmly. "But it seems like a lot of us had plans, when we were suddenly retired, that we hadn't necessarily shared those with the others."

"I wonder how much of that," Gage noted, "is because there's very little in the way of shields between us."

"Probably," Terk agreed, with a nod. "Everybody had temporary plans, though not necessarily anything long-term, and we were all planning on taking a holiday somewhere."

"Including you?" Gage asked Terk.

"Including me, but not in the same vein as you guys obviously," Terk noted, with a meaningful glance at Wade and Sophia. "I had planned to visit my brother and that whole group."

"Well, that's an interesting thing," Damon replied, putting down his fork and studying Terk. "That's where the woman was delivered to and all. So, what are the chances that somebody knew of your plans?"

Terk looked at him and frowned. "I hadn't considered that," he admitted in a very soft voice. "But you're right. If I had gone to Texas, Celia may well have been there at the same time."

"But does that mean we're dealing with two separate groups?" Tasha asked, with a frown. "One group doing something in terms of our *after-retirement* plans, and another group trying to stop us from ever having plans?"

"Another good point," Terk stated, as he sat back and looked at her. "We obviously still have a lot of answers to find."

"The trouble is," Tasha noted, "that all we're doing is finding more problems. Now that we have a prisoner, what will we do about it?"

"Interrogate him," Terk replied quietly.

"Does that mean kill him?" Tasha asked bluntly.

He frowned and looked at her. "We've never had to yet, not since the team was downed," he told her. "And I would hate to think that would be our only option."

"Good," Tasha said, her voice and her face relaxing. "I just didn't want to think that's where we were headed."

"I would hope not," Terk replied, "but, given the fact that these people are killing us and are after us even now, you need to be prepared for the potential that none of them will survive."

"I get that," she stated, "but that's a whole different story—not surviving during an attack versus not surviving because of interrogation is a pretty big difference."

Terk grinned. "You make whatever distinctions you need to," he suggested, "so that you can sleep at night. I'm all about finding out what the hell happened to all of us and making sure it doesn't happen again. And, if anybody has problems with that, you might want to reconsider being here." And, with that, he got up, and he walked out of the room. "I'll send Merk in to get some food, so make sure you leave him some."

Lorelei looked over at Gage and whispered, "Do you guys normally kill prisoners?"

He shook his head. "Nope, we have other methods."

She winced at that. "I think I'll skip being a part of that, if you don't mind."

"Didn't expect you to be here," he added cheerfully, "but you wanted to come. Remember?"

"I know. I got it," she admitted. "Is there anything I can do to be useful?"

"Keep doing your job for one," Gage stated, "so you can maintain government access. And make it seem like you're alive and well."

"Well, I am alive and well," she confirmed, "so I can certainly do that, as long as I have a laptop."

"Yours came along with you, so is that all you need?" he asked, his eyebrows raised.

She nodded immediately. "That's all I need."

"Perfect," he replied. "Tasha and Sophia have already cleared it, and we work off a VPN here. Do you want a desk or to work from bed?"

"Given my leg, I was thinking maybe the bed," she suggested, "if that won't upset anybody." She glanced around, and the two other women both shook their heads.

"Do whatever you need to do for that leg," Sophia and Tasha said in tandem.

"Perfect," Lorelei replied, settling back. "And do we have regular work hours or should I go get started as soon as I'm done eating?"

"Well, in your case, it would be whatever hours you typically work your job with the government," Gage stated, standing beside her. "The rest of us, it's more of a case that we work as we can, rest when we need to, and we all work together, sharing information, trying to find the answers we're looking for at any given moment."

"Okay, so while I'm in the database, is there anything you want me to source?" she asked Tasha and Sophia.

"Yes," they both replied. Sophia smiled and deferred to Tasha. "We have access to a lot of the government database but not everything, so no one notices us."

"I should have better access, but you guys are hell on wheels when it comes to hacking, so maybe not."

At that, Sophia laughed. "Sure, but, if we can go in legally, it keeps the heat off us for a little bit longer."

"True enough, so write me up a list of names, dates, or whatever else you're looking for," she suggested, "and I'll fit it in."

Merk arrived, picking up on the conversation in progress, and added. "We need you to monitor our upper-level bosses." With a nod at Gage, Merk loaded up a plate, and took off again. Within minutes Terk returned—to a barrage of questions.

Lorelei's eyes widened. "Like how upper-level? And who particularly?"

"Director of National Intelligence. Director of CIA. The CIA's military liaison and who that contact reports to. Anybody above Bob in the DOD. No need to go as high as the US president."

"Wow. You think they are our enemies now?"

"Don't discount any theories at this point. Just look for sudden resignations, promotions, deaths. I'll need that intel daily."

"I should be checking in and doing more work today for sure," she noted. "And I'll have to make up for all the lost time," she added, with a frown, "so I'll be working late."

"Don't trust anybody, Lorelei, but the people in this room, the other guys on my team and on Levi's team and even Bullard's team, as needed." Terk sighed. "Too bad we can't trust our contacts on the ground, so we're not privy to governmental gossip within the various related departments." Terk looked around the room. "I'll be in touch with Levi and Ice. You all keep feelers to the ground too."

"Well, let's get you set up then," Tasha told Lorelei.

As soon as Lorelei rose from the table, she stood for a moment, gripping her chair back.

"It's still bad, isn't it?" Tasha walked closer and gave her a shoulder to lean on.

"I took quite a hit," she muttered. "I thought I was doing better, but it seems like it's not going that well today."

"Sometimes it's just a wrong step to the side or being up and around more, even added stress," Tasha noted, with a big smile for Lorelei. "Some rest is likely the best answer for you."

"Yet how much rest is anybody getting around here?" she asked, as she looked around at everyone.

At that, Tasha nodded. "I know. I've been hearing the same arguments all the time, but it's hard for us to shut down because what will we do? It's not like you can just take downtime when in the middle of an ongoing op. It's all about making sure that we're doing the best we can and keeping each other safe. We've got to get the answers we need, so that becomes the priority."

Lorelei nodded at that. "Let's hope we get some answers pretty damn fast."

Sophia smiled. "Come on. Let's get you settled in your room." Slowly, with the help of the two women, Lorelei made her way back to her bed. Then the women brought in Lorelei's electronics. It didn't take long to get the networking set up.

Lorelei looked at her laptop and asked, "Now, do we have to find another stream of internet around here, in case anybody's checking?"

"Yeah, we've taken care of that. What you've got there is already encrypted, so you're fine," Sophia replied. "Nobody should be making pathways where they don't belong."

"Good enough," Lorelei murmured, then she settled down. When she looked up and saw that Tasha and Sophia were leaving, she asked, "What is Gage doing right now?"

"Probably talking to the prisoner."

She winced. "Good, I'll just stay right here then."

At that, Tasha laughed. "Don't worry, us too."

Lorelei nodded, then pulled her laptop closer, so she could get to work.

GAGE STUDIED THE prisoner with a jaundiced eye. He looked over at Terk. "These guys never make life easy, do they?"

Terk shook his head. "Nope, they sure don't." Terk crossed his arms and stared at the man.

The guy just stared straight ahead.

"Do you think he knows that everybody else connected with this is dead?" Gage asked Terk.

"I don't think he cares. He doesn't think it'll happen to him."

"But that's what they all say," Gage protested, "yet it happened anyway." He knew it wouldn't get through to this guy, absolutely no way. They never believed it would happen to them. Gage looked over at Terk, then shrugged and suggested, "Let's just leave him. He can't get out of here, so it's really not a problem. We'll just call to get him picked up."

"That might be a better answer," Terk agreed.

And, with that, they stepped out of the room. Once they were out of hearing, Gage asked, "You got any suggestions?"

"Lots," Terk said, his voice tight.

"If we leave this guy alive, that won't be helpful for us."

"I know," he muttered, "but I don't think you'll break him."

"And why is that anyway? Money? Loyalty?"

"I don't know. Did Ice ever get any idea who this guy is?" He quickly texted her, while Gage waited. When Terk got a response back with a name, he held it up for Gage to read.

He shrugged. "Joachim Neller," Gage repeated. "I don't know the name, do you?"

"Nope, but I guess we need to find out everything we can about him," Terk stated.

Just then Merk walked back toward them, having eaten a bite in the kitchen.

Terk motioned at him. "We just got an ID in from Ice for our prisoner." He held up his cell to show him the name.

Merk looked at it, then shrugged. "Not anyone I know."

"An awful lot of guys are out there we don't know about," Gage grumbled. "Probably a local hire."

"I know. Did you talk to him?" Merk asked.

"He isn't talking," Terk replied quietly.

"Can you do any of that voodoo mind stuff?" Merk asked.

Terk hesitated, then turned to Gage.

"I don't know," Gage said honestly. "If I was at full strength, maybe."

At that, Merk looked at him, frowned, and replied, "You guys are still really hampered by that main attack, aren't you?"

"Yes, and that's why they did it," Terk confirmed.

Merk nodded. "Is there any way you can recharge, or any way the two of you can do something together so that you're more powerful?" he asked. "Or maybe if you all joined in together? I mean, if I'm not making any sense, just ignore me," Merk said. "I really don't know how you guys do what you do. I just know you have unconventional abilities to do some of this stuff."

"Well, we can do quite a bit," Terk replied quietly. "A

lot of it is stuff that we never had a chance to perfect, but we were working on it. Gage here had all kinds of stuff he was working on."

"I was getting close to some of it too," Gage noted.

"Would anybody have known that?" Merk asked, spinning suddenly to look at Gage.

"No, I don't think so," Gage replied. "I didn't even tell anybody on the team."

"Okay, and you didn't tell a girlfriend or something along that line?"

He shook his head. "No, that's one of the reasons Lorelei is here. We were thinking that, after we were all done with this government work, we could reconnect and get to know each other," he explained. "Apparently we all had made plans similar to that, without discussing it with the others."

"And I think I know the reason for that," Terk replied. "It's because we're so close in so many ways that we tend to block off a personal part of ourselves and keep it private, not necessarily to keep anybody out but because the energy tends to flow in the direction of our focus, and we don't want our thoughts spilling over where they don't belong."

"Could it?" Merk asked.

"Well, it certainly could, yes. It takes a lot of focus to control both our thought processes, plus all the information coming to us from others, so it doesn't become public knowledge. And it's not the information becoming public that's the problem really," he added. "It's just very taxing to keep private things private, and that's not what any of us needs right now."

"Of course not. It sounds like you're all still struggling to keep everybody alive," Merk noted thoughtfully. "So this stuff you were working on, Gage. What was it that you can do?"

"Just taking the work we've already done and trying to magnify it," Gage stated.

"So, like, if you two combined skills, talents, and energy or whatever it is, could you rattle this guy's cage?"

"Absolutely," Gage said. "We could rattle him, sure, but how much is the question. We might rattle him enough to shake some information loose maybe, but that's not necessarily what would happen. We could also rattle him to the point where he could have a psychotic episode and be a nonfunctioning human for the rest of his life too."

At that, Merk's eyebrows shot up. "Okay, I didn't know something like that was even possible." He looked over at his brother. "And if people found out that was possible? ... Then what?"

At that, Terk stared steadily back at him.

"That's what we're wondering." Gage nodded. "Like, if the decision was made that we were just too scary to live."

"No offense, but my vote on that would be yes," Merk stated bluntly. "I wouldn't want to think that somebody out there could rattle my brains to that extent."

"Already people are out there who can do it though," Terk noted, his voice low and hard.

"Jesus, are you serious?" Merk asked.

Terk nodded. "In the Iranian group, when we were there to target them," he explained, "unfortunately that was part of our kill orders."

Merk winced at that. "And here we like to think that our wonderful government doesn't play assassination games."

"They don't *play* at anything," Terk stated quietly. "The Iranians were training these people to use against us."

"Of course we take out physical weapons first, but now

presumably somebody over there decided that you were also physical weapons and still a danger to them," Merk noted.

"That's the second working theory we have. The first is that our own government decided we were just too dangerous."

"I can see that one too," Merk agreed, shaking his head. "It's a well-known fact that the government only likes tools they can fully control. You'll need to get information on this guy."

"Tasha and Sophia are currently tracking down everything they can find on our guest," Terk replied, "but what we're really trying to do is cross-reference him to the other bad guys we've run into and see who they all had in common."

"If they even had anyone in common," Merk noted. "Generally that would be a tier above. They tend to always keep the lower workers down below, so that nobody can get too high in the group. Plus hiring locally to really lead to a dead end."

"Yeah, we've seen that all before," Terk confirmed, "and it sucks."

"It all sucks," Merk stated. "Do you want me to go in and have a talk with him?"

"Well, you could," Terk said, as he looked over at Gage.

"Do you want to give him a little rattle?" Merk asked Gage. "Not a big one, just a little nudge."

Gage snorted.

"Sure, don't mind me," Merk replied.

"Do you want to go in there and watch?" Gage asked Merk.

"Watch what? You or him?" Merk asked.

"Him. And give me a shout if it looks like it's too

much."

Merk's eyebrows shot up. He studied Gage intently for a moment, and then, with a quick nod, he disappeared inside the room with the prisoner.

Terk whispered, "Just a little nudge."

Right. Gage closed his eyes and let his energy drift toward the other room. He saw the prisoner sitting in the middle, studying the new arrival. Realizing that he'd already met Merk in the park today, Joachim seemed to relax a bit. Gage focused on the base of the prisoner's spine, where the white cord was. Rather than going inside and giving his brain a rattle, Gage grabbed that cord really hard and gave it one hell of a jerk. Then he let go.

Hearing a shout, Gage opened his eyes and stared at Terk.

Merk opened the door, and Gage looked in to see the prisoner sitting there, not screaming, but his mouth was open in complete shock.

"Ah," Terk shared a glance with Merk. "That was just a little rattle."

Merk stared at the prisoner in horror and then looked back at Terk, and, in a hoarse whisper, he added, "You guys did that?"

"Well, Gage did," Terk replied, studying his brother. "And it wasn't a big rattle."

"Well, I don't know what the hell that was," Merk stated, "but you make damn sure that you never do it to me."

"That's a given," Terk stated. "But, at this point in time, it's just an energy shake."

Joachim still stood on the other side of the room. He slowly came out of it, but terror filled his expression.

Merk looked at him. "Feel like talking now?"

He stared at Merk, his jaw working, and then he sat down hard.

"Was that a yes or a no?" Gage asked, with half a smile. They stepped into the room to join Merk, and, with the three of them all here, Terk crossed his arms over his chest, the same way Merk was standing, and stared at their prisoner.

Joachim finally nodded. "I don't know what that was, … but we've been told that you guys were pretty freaky."

"Yeah, well, especially when we're pissed off," Merk stated.

The man swallowed several times. "Are they really killing everybody?"

"They're all dead downwind of you," Gage shared, "but then you took out the one closest to you, so you're right in the middle of it."

"Yeah, but that was my order," he said. "He messed up, and that's never allowed."

"So, don't you think getting caught by us would be considered a mess up too?"

The guy swallowed. "I was hoping I had too much value for them to just waste my talents and wipe me out like that."

"What do you think now?" Merk asked.

"I don't know what to think," Joachim said, "and I sure as hell don't know what you just did." His voice increased in strength. "Maybe they're right, and you guys should be put down, like the dogs you are."

"Yeah, well, you were sure giving it your best out there."

He flushed at that. "It's war."

"Yeah? For whom?" Gage asked. "Our team wasn't in any war."

The other man shrugged. "As far as we understood, it's

war."

"And now that you know it's not?"

"Yeah, *you* say that," Joachim argued.

"Just who do you think you're really fighting here?" Terk asked.

"The US government," he replied immediately.

"Interesting, but you do know that we don't work for them anymore, right?"

At that, Joachim's gaze shuttered, as he thought about it. "But you did," he replied.

"We did, yes," Terk admitted, "and then somebody tried to completely annihilate our team."

"It was probably your own bosses," he said, with half a laugh.

"And it could have been," Terk agreed, "but then we also found you guys trying to take us out as well."

"Not all of you, just a few."

"And why just a few?"

"We understood only a couple survived the accident."

"The *accident*?" Terk asked in a hard voice.

The guy shrugged. "That's what we were told."

"So you're just taking out the survivors?"

He nodded. "Because we're at war, and we understood … what we were doing," he said, yet he hesitated on that last part. "But now I'm not so sure what the war was about or what side I'm actually on at this point," he added, "and it's not a very comfortable feeling."

"And for that I sympathize," Terk said quietly. "Particularly when some wars just aren't all that clear to begin with."

"Isn't that the truth," he muttered. "So are you guys going to kill me?"

"No, not at all," Terk replied. "Why would we? Your

guys will do it themselves."

He stared at him in shock. "So you won't keep me safe?"

"How can we spend our resources keeping you safe, when all you're doing is killing off our team?" Terk asked. "And if they take you out, doesn't that ultimately help us?"

The guy swallowed again. "That's not fair. I told you everything you wanted to know."

"That discussion has not even started," Merk stated, as he pulled up a chair, then twisted it around and sat on it backward. "But if you want to tell all," he noted, "we might make a deal."

The guy looked at him, then at the other two. Finally he opened his mouth and said, "Honestly, I don't know a whole lot. We were told that several people were not supposed to survive an accident but did, and, if we went to the park, we could take you out there."

"So you didn't have anything to do with drones?"

"Drones?" he asked. "No. I don't know anything about drones."

At that, Gage settled back, realizing this was probably a completely different group, hired to take them out in case of a failure on the other side. "Jesus," he muttered. He looked over at Terk. "Do you believe this?"

"Unfortunately I do," Terk replied. He backed out of the room, looking at his brother. "Let me know whatever you find out."

"Will do," Merk noted. "We'll get everything he has to share. Not sure if it'll do much good though."

"Every bit helps," Terk added. But fatigue filled his voice, along with a frustration almost bordering on depression.

Gage watched his boss and friend walk from the room,

and he looked over at Merk. "He's really struggling with this."

Merk nodded.

"We all are, really. We're close, and, when you find out that you're being assassinated and that you don't even know what you did, well, it just brings out the worst in everybody."

"It does indeed." They turned back to Joachim, who stared at them.

"You really don't know why?" the guy asked.

At that, Gage shook his head. "No. We really don't know why."

"Well, that sucks." Joachim shook his head. "I mean, at least if you'll die, you want to know why."

"Exactly," Merk agreed, rotating his neck. "Now, what else can you tell us? How did they contact you?"

"Emails," he replied. "I get a phone call, saying there's a job to do, and that's it. Then I get the email with details of where you'll be. That's it." He shrugged. "There's nothing else to say."

"So you're a contract killer?" Merk asked.

"I've done a few jobs," Joachim said cautiously, "but nothing quite like this."

"In what way?"

"One was a pedophile, who got off with no jail time," he admitted. "I didn't mind doing that one. The guy abused and killed three kids. I mean, at some point in time, somebody has to take a stand."

"Why'd he get off?"

"One of the cops on the case was bad, so they had to throw out the charge."

"Of course," he murmured.

"And the other ones?"

"They were similar," Joachim noted. "I was hired by a woman, who'd been badly raped. It was one of twin brothers, and she didn't know which one had done it. The DNA exonerated both of them because they couldn't prove which one it was. She didn't know if she'd been raped by one or the other or both, so she hired me to take care of both of them."

"So you didn't care who was guilty or not?"

"At that point, no, I didn't really. Honestly, after tracking them for a while, I knew they were both assholes. I wouldn't be surprised if it hadn't been both of them, knowing that they could get each other off."

"Unfortunately just enough people are out there who manipulate the law in order to do something like that," Gage murmured.

Joachim nodded. "But you guys? I mean, this was the first of its kind."

"How do you feel about it now?"

"Well, I hired the guy I worked with, and then I had to kill him. If I didn't, then …" He just let his voice trail away.

"And you think he knew the score?"

"Well, I know he knew the score, but I don't think anybody ever expects it to go that way. No, I'm sure he didn't," he murmured.

"So, outside of emails, they contact you by phone?"

He nodded. "They gave me a burner phone, and you already took that one off me," he noted. "There's almost nothing but three words or less for notifications, like, *It's a go*, things like that. I've had a couple phone calls, but nothing more. It's been pretty simple," he added.

"So, how did the other contract killing clients get a hold of you?" Merk asked.

He smiled. "Honestly, it was just through the website."

"You have a website?" Gage asked, staring at him. "What is it? Assassins for hire dot com or something?"

"No, it's run through a broker," Joachim shared, "and he takes a percentage of my money."

"Well then, you would think that he might have known something," Gage noted.

"I don't think so," Joachim stated, "because it would cost him clients if these jobs were screwed up from the beginning."

"Quite true. Interesting," Gage murmured, as if he didn't know what to say. "And outside of these emails, do you have any other contact? Do you have a name or any idea what these guys are after in this job? The other contracts you did were all about retribution for injustices."

"Yeah, I don't know about the other guys. Maybe the same thing," Joachim suggested, "because that retribution is part of my motto. *If the law doesn't do it, I'll do it,*" he said, as if quoting something. "Did you guys do anything that you didn't get punished for?"

At that, Merk looked over at Gage, who just shook his head. "Nope," Gage replied. "And none of us work for the US government anymore."

"When you did though, did you do anything criminal?" Joachim asked. "Because that would be the only reason I would have gotten chosen for this job."

"No," Gage repeated. "You probably just didn't look at your client base all that well, and you accepted the job without doing the research to see if it fit the parameters of your morality level," Gage stated, with a snort.

Joachim shrugged. "You could be right, since a lot of money was involved."

"How much?"

"Over thirty million."

"Interesting. Just for today?"

"Yeah," Joachim confirmed, "just for today. It would be the score that would get me out of the business," he admitted.

"And it didn't occur to you that it might be the score that took you out instead?"

Joachim stared at him. "Are you suggesting that we were never intended to live?"

"That's an awful lot of money," Gage noted. "Why would they pay you that kind of money, when they could just kill you instead?"

He swallowed. "It did occur to me, ... but I was really hoping that wouldn't be the way it went."

"Maybe not, but you might want to reconsider it now."

"Now that I'm caught, it's hard to say," he added. "It depends on if you guys let me go someplace where I can get free."

"And where would that be?" Gage asked curiously. "As far as I can tell, no place is really safe."

"I have contacts," he replied quietly. "I can get out."

"And if we release you, then what?" Gage asked. "You'll just come back around for us with a second attempt?"

"No," he stated, "I won't. Next time around, you guys wouldn't let me live, would you?"

"Nope. We ever see you again," Merk noted quietly, "you're done."

"Got it," he said. "I just want to go."

"And where would we let you go?"

"Let me walk out the door, and I'll disappear to Paris," he stated. "I'm totally okay to just disappear, and I really do have connections there."

Gage hesitated, then looked over at Merk and shrugged.

"We'll have to talk about it," Merk replied.

"You'll need to do it fast," Joachim said. "I know that, if we failed, another team was moving in."

"Funny how you hadn't mentioned that yet," Gage said in a caustic tone.

"You didn't ask."

And something steady was in that gaze of Joachim's that made Gage believe him. "Any idea when?"

"As soon as they're given the word. If we failed, somebody else steps in," he repeated. "That's all I know."

"Do you know where they'll be coming from?"

"Nope, all I can tell you is that you won't see them coming. They're just the next wave. And behind that will be another and another after that."

"Unless we find the boss above it all," Merk murmured.

"Maybe." Joachim looked at Merk, frowned, and said, "Who are you and why are you here."

"Just a friend," Merk replied. "Just a friend."

"Well, you might want to change your affiliations then," Joachim suggested, "because anybody associated with these guys is on borrowed time."

As Gage started to leave the room, he turned back and asked, "Do you know anything about a woman being run down?"

The man looked at him. "Yeah. That was my buddy's op. He was the one I killed in the park today," Joachim confirmed.

"And why did he do it? Are you totally okay for him to have a separate job than yours?"

"Well, I didn't realize that he'd already hooked up with

these people."

"So it was the same group?"

Joachim nodded. "I think so. I know he hired on with me to do this job and hired another buddy of his to take on a second attempt because he failed on that one too."

"And that fail didn't get him killed?"

"It was the double failure that got him killed," Joachim noted. "But I know he did hire somebody to take her out. So if you're trying to protect her, good luck with that. It's already been paid for."

"So why is the guy completing it then?"

"Because he's trying to move up in that world, and he wants to make sure he can get his own jobs after this. Screwing people over isn't so good for business."

"And who is this guy?"

"I only know him as Bingo," Joachim stated. "It's a pretty stupid name, but that's all I know him by."

"And he's here in England?"

"Well, he is for this job, yeah, unless she's left already." Then he laughed when he saw their faces. "But of course she hasn't. Swear to God, you better put a double guard on her and good luck with that," he said. "Bingo is pretty desperate. He's cut his teeth and found that he likes the life, he likes the job, and he really likes the money. And there's a lot more where that came from." With that, he went silent for a bit. "That's all I'll say now." Joachim nodded. "You guys can decide what to do with me. I really hope you do the right thing. It would give me a chance to disappear and to do something different."

"We'll think about it," Gage replied, then he turned and walked out.

CHAPTER 4

WHEN HER BEDROOM door burst open, Lorelei looked up. She hadn't quite closed it as it was, but it was thrust wide open. Gage stepped into the room and stopped short, and she watched as what was clearly relief washed over his face. "Okay," she began, "that's not quite the reaction I was expecting when I saw you next."

He walked over, bent down, gently placed his hands on her cheeks, cupped her face, and kissed her hard. When he came up for air, she was gasping for breath.

"Definitely not the reaction I expected," she murmured, staring at him. "What's the matter?" she asked, looking bewildered. "You're acting like you didn't expect to see me here."

"And I'm not sure I want to see you here at all," he said, in direct contrast to his actions upon entering the room just moments ago.

She wasn't insulted, but she was terribly confused. "You want to explain that a little, please?"

He nodded. "You're in danger."

"I know that," she replied. "That's why we moved me here. Remember? So, what's changed?"

He winced. "It's not that anything has changed, but our prisoner has been talking."

"That's good, isn't it? So what was he talking about that

has you so wound up?"

"He just told us that, since the attack on your life failed, the original contract killer—who happens to be our most recent dead guy from the park earlier today—had already hired a friend to finish the job on you because he was taking on this other job to finish us."

"Good Lord," Lorelei said, "so I do have a killer after me." She stared at Gage in disbelief. "Why? How is that even a thing?"

"I don't know, but apparently it is," he murmured, as he sank down on the bed beside her. "So ... I got scared and just had that moment of 'Oh my God, they might have already got her,' you know?"

"Well, I'm not against the greeting just now"—she smiled—"and the reasoning behind it is a little unnerving at first, but I'm fine. And, as long as I'm here, I'll be safe."

He shook his head. "No way, you can't stay here," he murmured. "Anything can happen at any time."

"Maybe so," she noted, refusing to be pulled into his worry. "But you'll take care of me, and I know you can do that."

He frowned. "And what if I fail?"

"Sadly you will have to live with that regret for the rest of your life," she replied, "but I won't care because I won't be here." He stared at her as she shrugged. "I tend to get a bit fatalistic about the whole thing," she explained. "I mean, even when I worked for the government, it was something that I always knew could happen, but it wasn't something that I ever focused on. And I'm certainly not focusing on it now because honestly, it doesn't seem like something I want to waste my time and energy on."

"It's hardly a waste to reevaluate your life and to try to

be safe," he murmured.

"But how does any of this help me?" she asked. "It only really came home to me when I realized that the hit-and-run could have been somebody intentionally trying to take me out. It's an odd thought, but I've never mattered to anybody enough to be worth killing." As he stared at her, horrified, her lips twitched. "Yes, I'm making light of it," she teased. "Obviously I'll take this very seriously, and it is a little disconcerting."

"Of course it is," Gage agreed. Then he picked up her fingers, sliding his between them. "It is also something that I need you to take very seriously because anybody could be the next contract killer."

"Well, I'm sure you're online, tracking that guy you have in custody already, trying to find out who on his list of associates is connected and who else in this wonderful world of contract killers is involved," she noted. "So I'm in good hands. I mean, look at us. Between all of us here, we ran huge departments. We set up all kinds of missions and investigative cases and intel-gathering ops," she added. "I mean, this is hardly new for us. What's new is that we are the ones with targets on our backs, and we're trying to save ourselves this time, but we have all the skills we could possibly ever need. So we can do this."

He smiled, leaned over, and kissed her very gently this time. "How very true." Lifting her laptop off her lap, he asked, "Now, are you ready for bed?"

"Whoa, whoa, whoa," she protested. "No, I'm not."

He looked at her, and then he waggled his eyebrows.

"Oh, no, you don't." She laughed. "You don't get to just waltz in here and sweep me off my feet, thinking that'll be enough."

"Why not?" he asked. "It isn't enough?"

She was still laughing. "But, now that you are here, you can help me to the bathroom."

When he had completely cleared off her bed, he flipped back the covers and helped her to her feet, taking her to the bathroom door. "Call out if you need me. I'll be within hearing distance. Then I'll go have a shower."

She nodded, feeling some of the fatigue from earlier settle in now that he was back again. She hated to admit it but figured she had probably been waiting for him all along. She closed the bathroom door and quickly brushed her teeth, thankful she could bring her things from the hotel. She smiled at the thought and wondered at the events of the day. But then she knew she was in the best possible hands. So, whatever happened, it's all good. By the time she was done and headed back out, she felt shaky again.

He took a critical look at her, then nodded. "Yeah, it's definitely bedtime for you."

She rolled her eyes. "Stop being quite so protective."

"No can do," he replied, with a bright smile. "On the other hand, maybe being protective will keep you safe this time."

"Maybe," she murmured, then she slipped back into bed, wincing.

He asked, "Did they give you some painkillers?"

She hesitated, then spoke. "Yes, but I don't like taking them."

He shook his head, grimacing. "I think it probably would help you get a good night's sleep."

"But they make me so groggy in the morning," she murmured.

"You'll be fine," he said. "You'll be absolutely fine." He

looked in her things and brought out the medication for her.

She took half the dosage required, then snuggled into the bed. "Go have a shower," she mumbled, already feeling the fatigue hitting her. He disappeared into the bathroom. She laid here for a long moment, wondering what his plan was when he returned. But, as injured as she was, chances were he wouldn't do anything.

He also wasn't talking about the trouble with his own leg, which had seemed to get worse as the day progressed. Had he been injured in a way that he hadn't told her about? Thoughts like that stopped her from falling asleep. When he entered the bedroom with just a towel around his waist, she murmured, "How badly injured were you?"

"If you mean the leg," he replied, "that appears to be more of an energy glitch."

She pondered that for a moment. "Does that make sense to you?"

"Meaning that you don't know what an energy glitch is, right? Well, hey, welcome to our world. And, no, it doesn't make any sense to me, but it seems to be what we're talking about."

"Wow. Okay, so how do you fix an energy glitch?"

"Now Terk would say, *Time, energy, and healing abilities*," Gage explained, "but, in my case, I don't really know what's required. I keep trying to give it time to heal, but he would say it's probably connected to my own energy drain."

"And is that something you can heal?" she asked.

He looked at her, then nodded. "It is, indeed. It just may take a little longer than I thought."

She smiled. "In my opinion, we always think injuries take longer to heal than we thought."

He nodded, then walked over and shut down the light in

the bedroom. "Can you sleep now?"

"I think so," she replied. "I presume you're sleeping in here with me."

"Yep," he confirmed. "We'll be short on space as more guys get back, so I figured we might as well get used to it."

"Fine," she said, "and at least I know that nobody will slip in and slice my throat in the night."

"That is very true." Gage slid into the bed beside her. He shuffled gently, trying to get comfortable, and then he tugged her ever closer. "Now sleep," he murmured. "I promise that nobody will attack you in the night."

She wondered about that for a long moment and then realized, at least if they did attack, it wouldn't happen quietly, not with him around. She closed her eyes and slept.

IT TOOK EVERYTHING Gage had in him to be gentle and to let her sleep, but he could tell that she was still nerve-racked, upset, and emotionally overwrought. The last thing he wanted was their time together to be chased by terrible memories and fear. She was a hell of a woman. He'd always liked her, but, when they had met a while back, their relationship hadn't gotten quite as far as he would have liked. But, at the same time, it had been a connection he couldn't let go of.

He truly had been planning on seeing her after a short break, when the team had been disbanded. It blew him away how everybody seemed to have had a personal plan, but nobody had discussed it. He wondered at that and then realized it's because they were all totally okay with each other having a life, with each one of them doing something they thought was important, taking advantage of the time they had.

None of them had thought their team operation was over forever; it was just one of those things. A temporary setback. What they had together as a team was special, and nothing would jeopardize it. That was before they were attacked, of course. And now, hearing about how a contract killer had been sent after Lorelei had sent ice through his veins. He'd left the interrogation to Merk as soon as Gage could and rushed to check on her. Funny how he only recognized he really cared about somebody when he was in danger of losing them.

That she'd been attacked once was already too much, but to think of somebody being after her to complete the job, well, that was just mind-blowing. And definitely not something he wanted to contemplate. But he also needed to recharge pretty badly. Just not enough of that going on in his world right now. He closed his eyes, hating to admit that rattling the prisoner's chain had taken a whole lot more energy than Gage was happy to lose.

Energy should be something that he could recharge easily. It should be a process as natural as breathing, but, because of some weird synapse issues going on in his system right now, charging was not something he could do easily. He hadn't mentioned it to Terk, but he already knew that Terk understood something was going on and was trying to take it easy on him. Whatever *easy* could mean in this context. Because so much of it had nothing easy about it. But just at the point in time that Gage was almost under, he heard a knock on the door.

"Who's there?" he called out in a low voice.

It was Damon.

Gage slid from the bed, stepped to the door, and opened it ever-so-slightly. "What's up?"

"Are you okay to take a watch tonight?"

"Yeah, if I can get some sleep first," he confirmed.

"I'll give you six then?" Damon asked.

"That'd be perfect," Gage replied, and, with that, Damon disappeared.

It was a good idea, but it also brought out the seriousness of what they were up against. Gage slipped back into bed, knowing that his time was at a premium now. He closed his eyes, snuggled up close to Lorelei, and drifted off.

CHAPTER 5

L ORELEI WOKE IN the morning all alone. She stared at the empty spot in the bed, her heart feeling a sense of loss and sorrow. They needed time together obviously. Time that they wouldn't get anytime soon, but she had hopes for that down the road. She slowly got up, headed to the bathroom, and had the hot shower that called to her. She stepped inside, reveling in the wonderful feeling of the water flushing down her back and face. With her injured leg, she scrubbed as well as she could, being extra careful to make sure she didn't slip on the tiles or lose her balance. By the time she got out, dressed, and headed to the kitchen, she already felt a bit punchy.

As it was, Gage took one look at her, hopped up, and helped her to her chair.

"You don't have to help me," she noted. "I'm doing fine."

"*Uh-huh*, you don't look that fine."

She frowned. "I'm doing better than I thought, but that shower did take something out of me." He poured coffee for them both and brought it to her. She smiled, and then, when she smelled food, her eyes lit up. "Really glad to see you guys have some groceries here. I'm happy to have just a slice of bread and cheese, or, if you've got anything else, I'd eat that too."

At that, he retrieved a platter, warming in the oven, full of eggs and sausages, and a plate and silverware for her, setting it all before her.

She looked at it and smiled. "Okay, you guys have lots of food." She served herself and dug in.

He laughed.

Tasha and Sophia joined them. Tasha looked over at Lorelei. "Good morning. Did you work any last night?"

"I got a lot of it done, actually." She nodded. "I hadn't realized how behind I was, but I did manage to catch up. Now that it's Friday, hopefully nobody will be checking up on my work until Monday," she added, with a bright smile. "So, if you need me to do other work, just call on me."

"Well, since Ice ID'd our latest two shooters via facial recognition software, we've been going through all the known associates between the various attacks we've had so far," Sophia explained. "We have found connections between the two shooters in the park last night—our prisoner, Joachim, still in custody here, who killed his buddy, the other shooter, Walter Woods—to the three dead IT guys, Rodney Godwin, plus his brother Randall Godwin, and the kid, young William Poma."

"But we have one new name that we don't have any connection to that we're hoping goes upstream," Terk added.

"The second hitman after Lorelei," Gage noted.

"We have to make sure we remember he's unaccounted for too," Lorelei murmured.

"Right, we need to focus both on those above these hired guns in the hierarchy and whoever it is who's after Lorelei down below, the active killer on the ground," Terk murmured. "What was his nickname? Bingo or something?"

"Yeah, that was the name, Bingo. Apparently he picked up the contract to fulfill it and to build his reputation," Gage added. "Yet we currently have no idea who he is."

"I did a search while I was on watch last night," Terk noted, "but nothing popped."

"With a name like that"—Tasha shook her head—"either not a whole lot will pop or way too much will show up and not related to our matter. Especially if he's not well-known. And, if he's trying to build a reputation, that's even more likely to be true. He could be a total unknown."

"Yeah, and that makes it worse," Gage stated, "because it could be anybody." They all nodded at that. He looked over at Lorelei, smiled. "But she's here, and she's safe."

"That I am," she said, "and thanks again to you all for taking me in."

"No thanks necessary," Terk replied quietly. "We're all part of the same team here."

She smiled at him. "Even if we didn't realize just how much our lives are interconnected?"

He nodded. "Sometimes it takes crap like this to prove how truly connected we are." He got up and looked over at the others. "I need to see if our prisoner left."

"You don't need to." Gage shook his head. "He had already gone when I got up for watch." The women looked at him, frowning. He shrugged. "Terk wanted Joachim to have an opportunity to escape, if he so wished, and he took it."

"Good enough." Tasha sighed. "Although he knows where we are though. Still this way makes it easier for us, doesn't it?"

"It does, indeed," Terk agreed, "particularly when we don't have that same government protection behind us anymore."

"Agreed."

Just then Terk's phone went off. Standing here, he looked down at the screen. "It's Merk." He answered it. "What's up?" he asked, then his eyebrows shot up. "I'm putting you on Speaker." They all heard Merk's voice coming through the phone.

"Your prisoner? I just found him. Faceup in a ditch, with a bullet hole in the center of his forehead."

"Crap." Tasha sank into her chair. Lorelei looked over at Gage, her eyebrows raised.

He smiled wearily and shook his head. "We didn't do it, and he had every chance to stay with us. We warned him what would happen if he did leave."

"Of course you did." Then Lorelei shook it off. "And really it would have been pretty damn hard to keep him safe if they were seriously after him."

"Without the support facilities that we could have used, yes," Terk agreed. "It would have been damn hard, but we would have tried our best. However, he chose to leave," he reminded her.

Tasha nodded. "I get that. I'm just sad because, yet again, we have another death involved. It seems like we have very few answers, and nothing is going our way."

"And we get that too," Gage replied. Terk was still talking to his brother on the phone, privately now. Gage exchanged a glance with Damon, then turned to Lorelei. "Eat up, and then we'll go get some grocery shopping done. But not you, not with that leg, not to mention a price on your head."

"Well, I wouldn't mind getting out and getting some fresh air," she noted quietly, "but probably won't happen for a while, will it?"

He smiled at her gently. "Nope. We just can't risk it."

"*Great.* How long will that be?"

"Don't know," Gage replied, "but we have to ensure we give it long enough."

Lorelei looked around at the team gathering around her, wondering at the camaraderie, seeing a tribe with all the same mentality. Just then, Gage lifted his head, alert to something. Damon turned to stare at Gage.

Damon got an unfocused look on his face. "You're right." He nodded. "We have somebody here."

"Here?" Lorelei gasped. "What do you mean by *here?*"

But Damon didn't answer her. He slowly got up, and she watched the weird look on his face.

Terk asked, "Can you get a line on it?"

"I'm working on it," Damon replied quietly, but it was obviously hard for him to talk at the same time.

Lorelei looked over at Tasha, who was immediately on her feet beside Damon.

"Can you tell us who, what, how?" Tasha asked Damon. When he didn't reply, she turned to look at Wade. "What about you, Wade?"

He nodded. "A new signature, not one we've seen before."

"Of course it is," Lorelei replied, feeling trapped. "There appears to be no end to this."

"Isn't that the truth?" Sophia agreed. "I'm on it though." And she bolted to the computers, Tasha on her heels. Not knowing quite what to do, Lorelei just sat here and watched. She slowly continued to eat, not sure if the women were coming back anytime soon. If this was major, and they would have to run, Lorelei didn't know what to do, and the guys weren't talking, at least not to her.

Regardless, it's like they were all speaking a language she didn't know or understand. It was frustrating, though it was also unique, quite fascinating, and she hoped that she could learn more about it. But, at the moment, it just seemed to be completely foreign to her.

It was really hard to figure out just what she was supposed to do, and that wasn't normal for her. Generally she was a busy person and was heavily involved with anything that went on around her. But this time, wow, she just continued to eat, watching, unsure if she should even be eating, thinking that her stomach might revolt at any second. But it's what she could do, and she needed the nutrition, so she was doing it. Finally she put down her fork, shoved away the plate. "If there's anything I can do to help ..."

But nobody responded. She frowned and sank a little lower in her chair.

Feeling useless was not an experience she was terribly used to or comfortable with. She at least had her laptop, and she could monitor some emails and see if anything was coming through the normal CIA and FBI channels. She headed to her room and picked up her laptop and brought it back to the kitchen. There she sat down and took a look to see if anything was coming through.

But her access had been denied. Frowning, her heart sinking, she picked up her encrypted phone and called her new boss. When he answered, she asked, "Hey, what's going on?"

"Oh my goodness," he replied. "What are you doing?"

She stared at the phone. "What are you talking about?" she asked. "I worked for hours last night, doing stuff for you, and this morning, when I went to log in, I can't get in."

He explained, "I'm sorry. I'm the one who issued that

order, but I was told you were dead." There was shock in his voice.

"Well, I'm not dead," she stated. "Your intel is wrong. Who the hell told you that?"

At that, she looked up to find Gage standing beside her, a frown on his face. She shrugged in a helpless motion and put her phone on Speaker.

"Could you please confirm who told you that?" she asked. "As you can hear, I'm definitely not dead. I'm perfectly alive and well."

"I don't know what's going on," her new boss said, his confusion evident. "Don't get me wrong. I'm absolutely overjoyed that you're okay, and obviously I'll get your access restored. I just would like to know what the heck happened with that intel. That's not exactly something you want to get wrong."

"No, it isn't," she snapped. "Believe me. At the moment, you've got me a little more than spooked too."

"I'm so sorry," he said. "Obviously that's the last thing I'm trying to do." She wasn't sure who was trying to do what at this point, but none of it was making much sense. "If you'll restore my access, that would be great," she repeated quietly. "And maybe do an investigation to find out who erroneously reported my death," she snapped. She was trying to be nice about it all, but this shit was unnerving.

"Of course, of course. I'll get it done right away." He hung up, and it took another ten minutes before all her access was restored again.

She looked over at Damon. "Nobody is talking about what happened, but I do have access again."

"I wonder if that was a test," Damon offered.

"What kind of a test?" she asked, looking over at Terk.

"To see if the job had been completed."

"And now that they know it failed?"

He nodded.

"*Now* they know it failed." She winced. "That's not exactly how I want to look at this either," she muttered.

"Of course not." Terk nodded. "The fact of the matter remains that we do still have a fairly big problem going on here," he murmured. "We need to get to the bottom of it."

She nodded. "It would be awfully nice if people would leave me out of this equation."

"Do you see that happening anytime soon?" Terk asked, with a smile.

Shaking her head, she replied, "No, but I could hope."

He laughed. "Now that you have access, you might want to see what they were trying to keep from you."

"I'm already on it." Her fingers flew, as she swiftly moved through any of the updates that had happened in the last few days.

"Do you have full access?" Gage murmured.

"It will take me a little while to sort that out, but I'm checking," she noted. Several minutes later, she called out, "It looks like full access was restored, but it is still very unclear exactly what happened. I've also been texting my old boss, and he doesn't know what happened either. He's looking into it."

"Of course he is." Gage gave an eye roll. "Like they don't know already what one hand is doing."

"I've got to wonder how much of it was simply something like," Damon added, "they were assuming or hoping she was dead, but now that they know she isn't, they'll ramp up the attack."

"Well, if it were me," Wade noted quietly, "I would."

She looked over at him and winced. "You know that's not what I want to hear right now," she snapped.

He gave her a ghost of a smile. "Of course not, but we can use all this to our advantage. The bad guys now know you're alive and well. Did you tell your boss you were still in the hotel?"

"I didn't tell him anything," she replied.

"Good. That'll work to our advantage too," Gage noted. "If they don't know for sure, they'll have to check."

She nodded but wasn't exactly sure who and what and where they would check. "Do you think they'll go to my apartment or my hotel?" she asked.

"Both probably," Gage said bluntly. "They don't know where you are, and they can't let it go, without finding out for sure."

"And if they can't find me?"

He looked at her and nodded. "That's the question, isn't it?" he asked. "Because, if they can't find you, they'll have to figure out why and how you got to wherever you are now. So we need to anticipate how they'll change that status quo."

"And will he call me back, or is that all the games they'll play at this level?"

"I'm not sure." Gage shook his head. "Yet calling you back doesn't really give them much, does it?"

"I'd like to think it doesn't give them anything," she snapped. "But, of course, it does give them something, doesn't it? Otherwise they wouldn't have done any of this."

"Exactly," Gage murmured. "And the sooner we find out what game is being played, the sooner we can put a stop to it."

"Wouldn't that be nice?" she muttered.

Just then her phone rang. She looked down at it,

frowned. "It's him, my old boss."

"Good," Gage replied. "Keep him on the line while we trace him."

"He should be at the office." She answered the phone, and her boss, now with a jovial tone, said, "Just so you don't worry, from what I can gather, some other woman died, carrying your ID, and that's why they thought it was you."

"Interesting, … since I'm both alive and still have my ID," she snapped.

Silence came on the other end of the line. "You have all your IDs?" he asked.

"Yes, at least I think so."

"Well, I suggest you check that," he stated. "Maybe you had a friend who stayed over, and maybe she decided to borrow something." He emphasized the word *borrow*, and she winced at that.

"Okay. Fine. I'll check into it," she replied, "but I sure as hell hope you're wrong."

"I don't know that I hope that at all," he noted, "because what I'm really happy about is that it's not you." And, with that, he signed off.

She groaned. "Apparently a woman in the morgue is carrying my ID."

At that, everyone was spurred into action.

"If somebody in the morgue has your ID," Tasha stated, "we'll find it."

Lorelei then watched in amazement as the women quickly accessed a database that they shouldn't have been allowed into. But, as Lorelei was finding out, what was allowed was very changeable and apparently on a daily basis. Including her own access, and that was disturbing enough to keep her rattled. She looked over at Gage. "I don't understand," she whispered. "What can they gain by having me dead?"

"Well, out of the picture is one thing," he explained. "And that is obviously what they were hoping for. Though the fact that some other woman quite possibly did die in your place is definitely concerning. Do you have your ID?"

"You're not kidding, And I lost my purse – or maybe it was stolen considering this turn of events," she murmured. "Do you think she actually had my ID on her or that somebody misidentified her?"

"I'd go with the latter," Gage replied, "but I'll head to the morgue right now and see for myself."

Lorelei immediately stood up and said, "No, I don't think that's a good idea."

He looked over at her, smiled. "Maybe not, but we've got to start getting some answers, so I'll check it out."

She groaned. "You know it's not smart."

"Doesn't matter if it's smart or not," he noted cheerfully. "We have to get to the bottom of it. I need to know if somebody is there and who provided the identification."

She frowned at that. "Do you have to go in person?"

"Pretty much," he murmured.

"I don't like it, Gage," she repeated. "Anybody who's looking for me will be seen. If the bad guys don't know you're alive, no sense in telling them."

At that, Gage frowned, as Terk laughed and added, "She's got a good point there, you know?"

"Well, I was looking at doing another disguise anyway." Gage looked over at Lorelei. "How's your leg?"

"It's fine," she lied.

He snorted at that. "Glad to hear it. Do you think you're up to helping me dye my hair?"

She looked at his dark blond hair and nodded. "What

will you do with it?"

"Add red streaks is what I was thinking."

"Okay, fine," she added, "but what about the beard?"

"It's fake," he explained, "and I'll change it the next time I go out."

She nodded slowly. "I hadn't even noticed."

"Good," he stated, with a big laugh. "That just means it works."

By the time they were done with the dye job, he looked completely different yet again. Because he had just removed his beard, his skin looked pale and matched the red in his hair quite nicely.

"Do you really think you should go?" she asked again.

"I do," he told her. "You for sure can't show up, as there is a good chance the bad guys could be watching the morgue too."

She stared at him. "Why would anybody watch the morgue?"

"To see if you show up," he explained, laughing.

"Well, that doesn't make any sense."

"Nothing these guys do makes any sense, but, when somebody close to you finds out that you're not dead, and they come to check on who is dead, it stands to reason the person asking these questions knows something about this poor woman's death and something about you."

"See if you can identify the woman who's there at least," Lorelei suggested.

At that, Sophia piped up. "There is a woman in the morgue under your name. No autopsy done, hit by a vehicle one week ago." Sophia looked over at Lorelei. "When did you get hit?"

"It was longer ago than that," she replied. "So they obviously took a second shot and maybe got the wrong woman or something." Lorelei was sick to her stomach at the thought. "Good God, do these guys really have no sense of right or wrong?"

"No, they absolutely do not," Gage stated clearly. "And that's what you need to remember too."

She frowned at Gage. "I really don't like the idea of you going."

"And I don't like the idea of somebody hunting you, but that also means that second attempt was made after you got hit but before the two shooters at the park died."

"Yes, but maybe it was one of the shooters at the park who made the second attempt," Terk suggested.

"It's quite possible that was a second attempt at killing Lorelei," Gage stated, thinking out loud, "and realizing one of the park shooters didn't have time to keep playing around, he hired somebody else to do the job." And, with that, Gage was gone.

Lorelei turned toward the rear exit door. "I don't like being stuck here," she announced to anyone who would listen, which was followed by a couple random chuckles around her.

Tasha looked over with a commiserating expression and nodded. "We know, but, for the moment, until you're healed up and more mobile, it's the best place for you."

Lorelei's shoulders sagged. "Sure, I know. Is there anything I can do to make myself useful then?"

"Keep doing what you're doing to make it appear like all is well in your work world," Terk advised. "It'll change fast enough."

She stared at him. "What'll change?" she asked.

"Your status at the office."

She took a long deep breath and let it out in a heavy exhale. "Meaning, that he'll hear that I've been killed after all?"

"Well, that's their intention, I'm sure," Terk murmured, "but obviously we'll do everything we can to not let that happen."

She quirked her lips at him. "Thank you for that. I'd really just as soon not die at this point in my life."

"None of us want to," he added in all seriousness. "And, in order to keep everything happening as it needs to be," Terk stated, "we all need to cooperate. So your job is to maintain the status quo and to not let anybody know something's wrong."

She winced. "Got it, even though definitely something is wrong."

"Of course," he agreed, with a bright smile. "But the less they know at work, the better."

She nodded, bent her head to her laptop, and went to work.

AS IT HAPPENED, Wade had decided to come along with Gage, even though Wade stayed in the truck.

"You know that you're too weak," Gage stated. "You should have stayed at the compound."

"Well, if we both were in any better shape, we wouldn't both need to be here," Wade argued. "You need some backup, and I'm better than nothing, right?"

Gage frowned at that, then shrugged. "I get it. I mean, I really do. I'd just rather have you back there, protecting the warehouse instead, but, when we're all spread so thin, it's hard."

"Just go." Wade waved a hand at the morgue. "See if you can get a read on who they've got in there, on who could pass for Lorelei."

"That would be nice to gather some intel. I've got a little bribery money on me."

"You know they say that bribes don't work with them." Wade chuckled.

"Which is total BS," Gage murmured, "as we know."

"Definitely."

And, with that, Gage headed out. Once inside the building, he found the morgue and dealt with the tech still on duty.

"We don't have anybody like that," he replied.

At that, Gage gave him a hard stare. "Look," he began. "She works for the government, and they've already been contacted to say she's passed on. We know for a fact that she hasn't, so we need to see the body to find out if they're trying to do something funky."

"It's the government," he noted, raising his hands. "They're always trying to do something funky." Shaking his head, he added, "Well, what do I care if you want to see a dead body? Just don't do anything funny with it, okay?"

Gage stared at him, hating that he even suggested such a thing. "I think I can restrain myself," he said in a tight voice.

The guy rolled his eyes. "Fine. Come on. It's right down here." Once inside the room to hold the dead, he opened up one of the drawers and pulled out a tray. Lifting the cover of the sheet off her face, Gage stared down at a decent facsimile of Lorelei, in the sense that she had the same fine cheekbones and nose and the same long brunette hair, yet with road rash running down the side of her face.

Gage nodded. "Not wanting to piss you off or anything,

but I need a picture, so I can see whether anybody can ID her."

"As far as I'm concerned," the tech replied, "she's already been ID'd."

Gage looked at him and asked, "So you'll let an incorrect ID stand?"

"I don't have any reason not to," he argued.

"Even though I've just told you that it's not the right person?"

"Well, that's for the investigators," he noted. "I'm just here doing my job, and I'm not changing anything until somebody tells me to."

"Good enough," Gage stated, suddenly cheerful. "That works for me."

The guy looked at him, frowning.

Gage shrugged. "I have to assume that somebody is possibly trying to kill the real woman with this name, so, if you leave it as is, they'll think she's dead."

The guy shook his head. "You government guys can play your spy games, but it's got nothing to do with me." With that he closed the drawer and took off.

But Gage had his photos, and that was worth everything. With the tech gone, he looked around for a few moments and then opened up another drawer or two, wondering if something else was going on here that he wouldn't have expected.

He really had no business opening up these other drawers, but, when he got to the third one, he found the shooter from the park, the one who Joachim Neller killed in front of them. Gage quickly took a photo of him, closed that drawer too, and then headed out.

Back in the truck, he handed over his phone to Wade.

"I've got photos. One of the dead pseudo Lorelei, which the tech refuses to claim as a false ID, not until investigators confirm it. Then beside her in the morgue drawers was the idiot from the park, Joachim's partner who he promptly killed. Got his photo too."

"Really? Well, I guess it makes sense that he's there. Where else would they take him?"

"I know, but I have to admit it was a bit of a surprise though."

"That's all right. We get used to these surprises, whether we like it or not."

Gage smiled at that. "*Very* true. Still, it's a fairly decent likeness to Lorelei, and I presume the poor woman didn't even know what hit her."

"I would imagine that's quite true," Wade agreed, "and, if you think about it, it could have just been a case of mistaken identity."

"She's young," Gage noted sadly, "and cut down in her prime for no other reason than that she resembled somebody else."

"Which seriously sucks for her."

"I know, yet what are we supposed to do about it?"

"Nothing we can do. It's definitely not the one that we're looking at though, right?"

Gage looked at him. "What do you mean?"

"I know it sounds wrong, and this might piss you off, but I just want to make sure that there's no dead ringer here. You really do know what Lorelei looks like, right?"

Gage stopped, stared, and then swallowed. "Wow, you know what? I hadn't even considered that. It would be damn smart on their part, if that were the trick, but, no, we've definitely got the real Lorelei back at headquarters."

"Good," Wade said, with relief. "Sorry for having to bring it up."

"No problem. Hey, if that thought crossed your mind, the best thing we could do is deal with it right off the bat. And, man, you know, if it wasn't a case of having already known her, that could have been a legit risk, exposing us all to disaster."

"And we just don't know what else might be going on in this world. It's all gone crazy, it seems. So now what are we doing?"

"I guess we head back." Gage slowly pulled out and then thought about it and added, "While we are out though, we might as well pick up groceries."

"Seems like we constantly need to pick up groceries." Wade laughed. "So that's what's next then. I'll give Sophia a call and see what we need to pick up," After a quick discussion, he easily made a list and looked over at Gage. "Need to find a grocery store."

"Right, and we need a big one, I'll bet. Plus, I suppose Tasha will be looking for fresh bakery bread again." Gage smiled.

"She's always looking for bread apparently," Wade murmured. "Bread and the fixings, like cheese. She's more French than the French."

"I don't know," Gage argued. "I don't think I'm man enough to say that to her."

At that, Wade burst out laughing. "No, I can see how that wouldn't necessarily make her happy."

The two men grinned, sharing a light moment. However, as Gage pulled out onto the main street and started driving, he kept checking the rearview mirror.

"What's the matter?" Wade asked.

"I'm wondering if we've picked up a tail."

"Oh, I hope we have," Wade noted in delight. "It would be nice if we finally had somebody show their hand. I'm about sick of these assholes."

"Hey, they've been showing their hand constantly, but the trouble is, they're getting ahead of us and killing off everybody, long before we've had the chance to even get near them."

"At least we got some intel off Joachim before they killed him too," Wade noted.

"Right. Before we've had a chance to do much of *anything* at this rate. The most frustrating part is trying to get ahead of these guys, and that's not working too well."

"No, it isn't, but, hey, we'll get there."

Gage drove around town and headed to the grocery store. "No reason for them not to see us buying groceries."

"Except for the sheer amount that we need to get," Wade muttered.

"Well, there is that. But we also aren't getting everything here."

"No, we'll have to make several other stops." Together they went into the grocery store and bought a cartful. When they came back out, Wade lifted his chin. "Look. The vehicle is still there."

"Good. You got a license plate?"

"Yeah, I already sent it to Tasha, when we went into the store."

"Oh, good," Gage noted. "I wasn't at the right angle."

"Well, I was, and, now that we're back outside, I'm hoping for some answers."

"Well, let me know if they say anything." Gage hopped in their truck. "Otherwise I'll carry on with our grocery shopping." He shook his head. "Who knew we could eat so much food? We are burning through a lot of energy though," he muttered.

"And we have injured people," he reminded him.

"I know. I know. Especially right now." He looked over at Wade. "How are you doing?"

"I'm doing okay," he replied, "but I should be asking you that."

"I'm doing okay physically," Gage noted, "though the leg is still bad in terms of mobility, but I'll ignore that for the moment."

"Yeah, let me know how that works for you," Wade teased, but he was keeping an eye on their tail, while Gage pulled out of the parking lot and drove to their next stop.

"It works fine. At least it has worked fine so far," Gage corrected. "After this, I don't know. Have you put any thought into what happens after this?"

"Well, I had plans before, but that got blown all to hell," Wade shared, "so now I'm not so sure what *after this* even means."

"Did you ever think that maybe we should set up our own company?" Gage asked.

Wade stopped what he was doing, which was going through his pockets and sorting through his lists, then stared at his friend. "Did Terk mention that?"

"Not yet," Gage noted, "but you've got to know he's thinking about it."

"Yeah, I imagine he has," Wade agreed, "and it's an interesting thought. I won't say no because I really don't know what I'll do after this. We had retirement dangled in front of us, which was interesting to think about."

"Yeah, but what were the chances of you actually retiring?"

"That's true, and honestly, I've had several business proposals offered to me."

"Me too. I'm guessing we all have," Gage guessed. "Were there any that you jumped on?"

"No, I didn't. I had figured I'd take a break and really think about what I wanted out of life and would decide what came next later. Then things happened so fast," Wade added, "I didn't even really get a chance to figure out what I wanted."

"Same here," Gage agreed. "But I just couldn't quite believe that I wouldn't be working with Terk anymore. Honest to God, we have grown so much through our association with him that it's just mind-boggling to think Terk's company won't still be there."

"Yet, if we were to set up our own company, we—"

"I know," Gage interrupted. "Have you ever wondered just what the extent of our capabilities are?"

"Of course I have," Wade replied briskly.

"And sometimes I wonder how much we could do if we joined forces, which was something we were just starting to explore."

"Exactly, but we never really got very far, did we?"

"No, we didn't," Gage agreed, "but we never really had the time, but maybe now we could." The two men looked at each other. "Terk has a ton to offer," Gage stated.

"He does, but I think he's feeling a bit on the betrayed side right now."

"I can't blame him for that, but maybe we can help him with that a little bit. He just needs to know that the work he does is valuable and that we all appreciate him."

"We could probably all stand to hear that," Wade noted

quietly. "Nothing worse than finding out you've become redundant, when you didn't even know you were in trouble," he murmured.

"I expected that we might face that someday, but I wasn't ready for it by a long shot, if you know what I mean."

"I know exactly what you mean," Wade agreed. "And expecting it is one thing, but actually being told that you're done is another."

"It was a shocker, though people go through layoffs all the time. Still, with our work"—Gage gave a shrug—"well, maybe it's just egotistical of me, but our work is special."

"It *is* special," Wade agreed, "which is why your suggestion has a lot of merit. Particularly ... if we can add in the partners."

Gage frowned at that. "And then we'd have to trust a lot more people."

"We have to trust in order to let them into our lives and into our hearts anyway," he reminded him.

"I know. I really do. Just seems odd to extend it past the basic team."

"Do you trust Lorelei?"

Instantly Gage nodded. "More than a lot of people," he admitted. "I mean, our team was a godsend. But there were times that I even looked at Wilson and wondered every once in a while."

"That's just because he was different." Wade laughed. "But he was also brilliant, and that's a loss of life that shouldn't have happened."

"No, and Mera too. They were both really talented, and somebody needs to pay for that," he added, his voice gaining strength.

"Like how the hell is any of that fair? They weren't prepared for attacks like that."

"Nothing is fair, and we know that," Gage agreed. "I guess we should be counting our lucky stars that we didn't lose Tasha as well." His tone had turned brisk, while speaking of these losses within their extended team.

"Yeah, our whole team needs her and Sophia and Lorelei. On that happy note, let's get through the rest of this shopping." Wade rolled his eyes at the thought.

"Yeah, look at us, two tough guys, out shopping, just like some nanny or personal shopper or something."

"Get used to it," Wade teased. "Once you've got a partner, you'll be going shopping all the time."

Bursting out laughing, they carried on, first to the bakery and then on to the butcher. By the time they had everything loaded up, Gage looked over at his buddy and asked, "Did you get any update on the tail?"

"Nothing besides satellite confirmation that it's still on us, which we already know."

"I've got to wonder how much of this crap is our own damn government," Gage suggested.

"Well, it's the right kind of vehicle and a pretty standard surveillance operation."

"By the book, all right. I wondered that too, but why?"

"I would say because of Lorelei."

"The whole *she's dead but not dead* thing?" Gage asked. "Meaning, she's not only *not* dead but from somewhere came the message and an identification saying she was."

"Right, so somebody thought she was dead, now knows that she isn't, so are they looking for her, or are they looking for us?"

"Probably both, and I'm hoping nobody knows who I am," Gage noted.

"We sure picked up that tail quickly. It could be that they were staking out the morgue, and our appearance just made them curious. Or maybe that guy at the morgue set them off."

"And that's possible too, damn it," Gage replied. Looking around, he added, "We have to shake them now, so we can get our groceries home."

"You can do that," Wade agreed. "I definitely know you have the driving skills. Just try not to crash us in the process, okay?"

Gage snorted. "Why would I crash us at this point in time?" he asked his buddy. "Besides, I'm the best driver we've got."

Wade looked at him, and his lips twitched, then had bloomed into a full-blown grin. "Oh, boy, here we go again with that—though I suppose you're right, as long as we're not counting all the other stuff, like laws and speed limits and that sort of thing." Wade continued to smile.

As the two hopped into the vehicle, Gage drove off, racing through different parking spaces, twisting and turning, until he shook off the tail.

"I find myself wondering if we should have shaken off that tail," Wade added.

"Don't worry about it," Gage said, with a grin, "because I came around behind them."

Wade looked at him in surprise and then in delight, when he saw the vehicle up ahead. "Good Lord," he declared, "you're crazy. Now what?"

"Well, what are the chances that he'll lead us somewhere?" Gage asked. "I don't know about you, but I'm getting damn tired of being followed. It's about time for us to get ahead of these guys and go frontal."

"Well, going frontal is one thing," Wade agreed, "yet going full-frontal is a whole different story."

"Not to me," Gage argued. "These assholes have had us shaking our leg for a long time, and I don't know which one of them is responsible for killing off our admins, trying to kill off our team, but, damn it, I'm done with their shit, whoever it is. We still need the rest of our team back up and on their feet. I'm not sure how to make that happen either," he added. "I don't think Terk has any idea how to help the other guys, other than with more of his energy siphoned off to them and more and more time passing."

"I know, and he's not talking about it at all. Don't know if that is good or bad. Now there's two of us plus Damon, but the others are still down. Losing Wilson and Mera was a blow that Terk hasn't recovered from either. I feel bad for Tasha too, as she worked really closely with them as admins. Obviously they were considered to be a threat to someone."

"Damon mentioned she's taking it pretty hard. Of course those were the people she worked the closest with," Gage admitted quietly. "We were all part of the same team, but they were in her field. Their deaths hit close to home, almost taking her out too, so, of course, it's been pretty rough on her." He nodded.

"She's also pretty upset that they went back after Mera, I hear."

"According to Damon, if they had moved Mera, like they had tried originally, she would be alive right now. Terk had one of the last conversations with her too, so he is pretty upset about that. However, apparently Mera felt safer where she was, considering she'd been shot and didn't want to be on the run."

"Well, she might have survived if she'd come in, but, on

the other hand, maybe the others would be dead," Wade reminded him. "Who knows what would have happened. Just remember. One event changes another."

"I know, but trying to convince Tasha of that is a whole different story." And, with that, they pulled right behind the truck that had been following them. At that moment, the driver seemed to realize that he was now in a dangerous position, and he took off, pushing his vehicle as fast as he could.

"Interesting move," Wade noted. "It's almost like he didn't know who the hell he'd been following or something."

"Yeah," Gage agreed, "like he suddenly realized that we're following him, and he's now the one in danger. I get the instinctive reaction," he added, as he stuck with him. "It was a shit idea on his part to run though."

"Why do you say that?" Wade asked curiously.

"Because now we know that he's no professional and that he really was following us. And every bit of information is needed intel."

"We also have details on the vehicle," Wade stated. "Of course it was stolen."

"How long ago?"

"Overnight."

"Somebody needs to call it in," Gage suggested, with a grin.

"Oh, don't worry. I'm sure they're already on it," Wade stated. "Knowing Sophia, I wouldn't be at all surprised if we aren't on satellite and if they're watching how you handle this."

"Oh, great," Gage replied. "Terk will give me a royal talking too after this."

"Not if you don't lose our tail," Wade added, with a

chuckle.

"Well, well. Looks like word got out," Gage replied, immediately reducing his speed, as several cop cars converged on the vehicle up ahead, lights and sirens blazing.

"Yeah, the trouble is, I don't know that this guy would let himself get caught."

"No, I don't think so either. And he shouldn't be doing a stakeout alone anyway." Gage pointed, as the tail vehicle sped up, faster and faster, then lost control up ahead. They couldn't see much of the collision itself because vehicles were everywhere, cops in front and more coming up from behind. The tail vehicle flew into the air and came down hard, landing upside down. Gage pulled off to the side, letting the cops go flying past. "Damn. That's not quite the way I had hoped this would end."

"The last thing we need is more dead bodies." Wade groaned.

Gage nodded. "I do want to go take a look though. Stay here."

Wade looked at him and asked, "Where is it that you think I'll go anyway?"

"Doesn't matter," Gage replied, with a bright smile. "I'll be in deep-enough shit with Terk as it is, so I can't afford to lose you."

CHAPTER 6

LORELEI HAD WATCHED the chase from the satellite feed. "So does that mean we have another dead guy?"

"I'm not so sure." Tasha tapped the screen. "Look. We've got one person out and running."

"And a second one running," Sophia added, "but that one is based on our tracking, so that must be Gage."

"And one's still in the other vehicle," Lorelei noted.

"Probably Wade because he's not quite healed enough to be in a foot chase like that."

"Better not let him hear you say that," Terk suggested, coming from behind them.

"Oh, I know," Sophia murmured, "all that fragile male ego." He just looked at her with a flat expression, as she smiled sweetly back up at him. "Not yours of course."

Terk didn't comment but continued to stare at the screen. "Not sure what's going on right now," he murmured.

Just then Wade phoned Terk. "So the vehicle that was following us earlier has had a major accident," he explained. "Once the cops joined in on the chase, our tail made a run for it, and now looks like someone has taken off on foot."

Lorelei watched in concern, as the figure they believed to be Gage came closer and closer to the one running away. "Wow, he'll really capture him, won't he?"

"Well, I don't know if we should hope for that or not,"

Terk replied. "Gage is still not nearly healed either."

"Yeah, but he's a little touchy on that topic." She snorted. "As far as he's concerned, he's as good as new."

"He always is," Terk admitted quietly. "In fact, he's
much better than that. But he can't use as much of his
energy as he should. He can't use anything but brute force
right now, and he's expending a ton of his own energy."

"Meaning he'll crash and burn when he gets home," Lorelei suggested.

Terk looked over at her and nodded slowly. "That's a
good way to look at it, ... and he'll have to because he'll
need to recharge." Terk continued to watch the screen
closely, as it looked like Gage had nearly caught up to the
fleeing driver.

"Now what'll he do?" It was like watching a movie, and
yet Lorelei could see that the tension she felt was universal, as
they all waited for the climactic moment. "Good God," she
said, "surely he won't try to bring him down himself."

Just then they watched the driver jerk several times.

Lorelei gasped. "Oh my God, he didn't shoot him, did
he?"

"Nope, he wasn't even looking at him."

At that moment Gage was looking around, trying to find
the shooter. Then Gage bent down, placed a finger on the
guy's neck, and suddenly turned, as other people raced
toward him. With his hands up, he slowly pointed to show
that he had no weapon. The others raced forward and
checked out the man on the ground.

"Now he'll be trying to fast-talk himself out of this,"
Terk noted quietly.

"Shit. I gather that's the cops then?" Lorelei asked.

"Yeah, not only is it the cops but these assholes took out

their own guy on us again."

"Damn it," Lorelei muttered. "So now we don't have anything, do we?"

"Not unless they can find the shooter."

As they watched, everybody split up, except for the one man standing beside Gage and the dead man, and it looked like a heated argument was taking place.

But finally the other man relaxed, and Gage was allowed to leave.

"He's good at persuading, isn't he?" Lorelei asked Terk.

"He also would have to provide his ID and a reasonable excuse as to why he was there."

"Of course he was trying to help the police, right? Just a concerned citizen," Damon noted, joining them.

At that, Tasha hopped to her feet, walked over, and asked, "Hey, how are you feeling after your nap?"

"Like hell, but I'm alive, and I'm working, so it's all good." Damon gave Tasha a gentle hug. Watching them hug, Lorelei felt tears in her eyes. It seemed like this whole explosion mess had brought a completely different energy to the group. She caught Terk looking over at the couple, frowning. "Is there a problem?" she asked softly.

He shook his head. "No," he murmured. "It's good for him."

Yet she wondered at that, but then realized Terk had to be considering his own scenario back in Texas. She winced at that. "Do you think Wade is okay?"

"He's fine," Sophia replied, holding up her phone. "We're texting. He knows what happened, and he's waiting right now for Gage to return."

"Well, we do have all the information on the truck, but it won't be of much help since it was stolen," Lorelei noted.

"It's all a help in that we'll find out the location it was stolen from, and we can go from there," Tasha added.

That's exactly what they did, and by the time the guys drove back home again, the admins had mapped out the suspected pathway, showing where everybody had been and had come from.

When the guys started unloading the groceries, Lorelei stopped for a moment in awe, as she realized just how much food they had bought.

Gage took one look at her, then grinned. "Well, it looks like you gals eat a lot," he teased.

"We do." She nodded in agreement. "But I blame Tasha for most of that."

Immediately Tasha turned on her. "What is that supposed to mean?" she cried out. Then she looked at all the groceries and joined the guys in the kitchen. "Oh, yum! Thank you. I will live to work another day."

At that, the rest of them burst out laughing.

"And maybe you will too," Lorelei said, walking toward Gage and giving him a hug. "If you'd stop chasing down bad guys, you wouldn't burn through so much energy."

"Hey, it wasn't my fault," Gage countered. "I was hoping for a chance to bring one back and get more answers."

"Like that worked out so well with the last one." Lorelei smirked.

He nodded. "Right, but we did get some intel. I keep living in eternal hope that something will change, you know?"

She smiled. "Something probably will, but not necessarily in the way we want."

"Well, something needs to turn around," Gage stated. "What I did get was a photo of the latest dead guy at least."

Gage shrugged. "I have no idea who he is or anything about him, and I did hang around long enough for the cops to check for any ID, but nothing was on the body."

"Of course not." Terk shook his head. "That would be too simple. Let's get facial recognition moving on that photo." Almost immediately his phone rang. It was Merk.

"Hey," Merk greeted his brother through the Speakerphone. "Was that you guys?"

"Well, let's just say that our guys were being followed, so they turned that around to become the pursuers. When the cops joined in on the chase, the guy completely flipped out and crashed the vehicle."

"Damn it," Merk muttered. "Why is everybody such a noob when it comes to the cops? We could have used him."

"True, but, as Lorelei just said a minute ago, the last guy didn't give us much of anything either."

"Do we have a name?" Merk asked.

"Yep, we've already just sent it over to Ice."

"Good and—"

"Wait, no. Sorry, no name but we have a face."

"Well, we'll take that," Merk noted. "Hopefully Ice can run it through some database and see what pops up."

Shortly after he hung up, Tasha called their attention to her computer screen. "Hey, guys, have a look over here." And several photos of the same face were on her monitor.

"Wow, that was quick. Facial recognition picked up our tail guy right away," Gage noted.

"He's on Interpol's watch list," she replied quietly. "And they're not at all unhappy he's dead."

"Of course not," Gage replied.

Everybody stepped forward, including Lorelei, who stared at the face. "He almost looks familiar." She frowned.

They all turned immediately to look at her. She shrugged. "Hey, I added *almost.*"

"That just means that he's familiar to you," Gage explained, "but you're not yet sure how you know him, how to find that in your brain."

"Maybe." Lorelei was a little unnerved at the heavy attention. "But it isn't that easy to immediately figure it out."

"Of course not," Terk admitted. "But chances are, your brain will fill in the details, if you give it a chance."

She nodded. "Well, it needs to get on it." She then returned her attention to the groceries. Suddenly she stopped, looked back at them. "Wait. I feel like he may have been at the hotel."

"The hotel where you were staying?" Gage asked.

"Yeah, I think he was wandering the hallways there one day, with someone else. I may have even spoken to him," she added.

"Now that's interesting. I wonder who else you might have seen."

"I don't know." She shrugged, showing her palms. "I didn't see the pictures of the two guys at the park."

Swearing, Gage pulled out his phone and showed her the picture of their prisoner, plus the guy in the morgue. "This one is Joachim, who we had here for a while. This is his buddy, Walter, who Joachim shot at the park the other night."

Lorelei's face visibly paled when she looked at the guy in the morgue. "He was definitely at the hotel."

"Okay, so Joachim killed his buddy, Walter Woods, who was supposedly the first one who tried to run you down. Maybe Walter was with Joachim?"

"There was more than one," she remembered. "I think

there was like …" She stopped, looked at him, and said, "I'm not sure. … Three maybe? I don't know. I … this is kind of freaking me out."

"Just sit down and relax. Then close your eyes and see if you can figure out exactly what you saw and when."

"No. I don't need to—" As she looked around at all the faces, she could see there was no sense in objecting. "Oh, fine," she murmured. "Just let me head off to a private corner and think about it for a minute." And that's what she did.

When she opened her eyes, Gage smiled down at her. "Hey."

"Did I fall asleep?"

"You sure did." He chuckled.

She flushed, horrified. "Oh my God, why didn't you wake me? I'm supposed to be thinking of the guys at the hotel!" She yawned, and he nodded.

"You were supposed to think about the men in the hotel."

She nodded, matter-of-factly. "There were four of them. Those two, the two park shooters, the dead guy and another one."

"Any idea who the other one was?"

She shook her head. "No, I don't know. He's the one I didn't get a very good look at."

"Well, that man is probably the last one standing of the group, aka *Bingo*, who was hired to take you down."

She let out a breath. "That's a little unnerving because that still means one is left."

"Yep." Gage nodded. "Still one asshole out there, looking to shorten your lifespan."

"Not very nice," she murmured, "considering I didn't do

anything to him."

"Maybe not," Gage agreed, "but believe me. These guys really don't give a shit."

She nodded and smiled. "Well, I know you'll track him down, so I won't worry about it."

He stared at her and then chuckled. "That's a good way to look at it. At least then I know that you'll have other things on your mind and not that one."

"Yep," she agreed, "it's called trust." She gave him a cheeky glance. "And you did bring food, after all."

He rolled his eyes. "Gosh, between you and Tasha ..." As they returned to the kitchen area, Sophia was opening a lot of the food.

She looked up with a smile and said, "I hope you don't mind, but I'm starving."

Lorelei burst out laughing. "He was just commenting about how Tasha and I are always hungry, but, if you are too," she noted, "maybe it's just a female thing."

"Maybe so," Sophia agreed, with a big grin.

"We're certainly going through the food," Tasha added.

"We are, at that," Damon agreed. "Let's hope nobody else notices."

"Well, we have to eat," Tasha stated comfortably. "And, if people do notice, it doesn't automatically give them a reason to come attack us."

"Says you," Damon teased.

At that, she turned and looked over at Damon. "Didn't you say somebody was outside earlier? A new signature?"

He nodded. "Yeah, but they couldn't get in."

"So how did they even find us though?" Tasha asked.

"That I don't know," Damon stated. "And I also don't know if they told anybody."

"If they told anybody, then we can expect an attack on the warehouse at some point," Gage warned.

"Got it," Tasha winced. "It'd be really nice if we didn't get attacked for once."

"Wouldn't it?" Damon smiled. "But I'm not really sure that I see that happening."

"*Great*," Tasha muttered. "Fine. Then let's eat, just in case they come and try to interrupt our meal."

"Hang on a minute." Damon laughed. "Are you more worried about losing out on your meal or on the attack?"

"Losing out on the meal of course," she snapped, immediately followed with a big grin.

He gave her a long hug, and, choking back a laugh, held her close and then added, "Come on. Let's get some food and then get you to bed."

"Hey, I just woke up," she protested.

"Yep, and by the time you've eaten," he noted, "you'll be ready to crash again."

Tasha nodded, but so did Sophia and Lorelei.

Lorelei was so tired. All the revelations of the men at her hotel had sunk it, zapping her energy. It didn't take long before it was all she could do to keep her eyes open. By the time she'd finished eating, she tried to help clean up but was immediately pushed in the direction of bed.

"Go on. Get to bed," Gage said. "I'll be down soon."

Too worn out to object, she waved good night to everybody and slowly made her way back to the room. She heard the chatter of conversation behind her, beginning with Terk's voice.

"How is she doing, Gage?"

"She's getting there," he replied. "I think she's in more pain than she's letting on, which is exhausting all by itself, but she's also doing too much, considering her injuries, not unlike a few others around here."

"That's the thing," Tasha noted, "everybody is. We're all trying to pull our own weight and more, but it takes its toll."

"Agreed," Terk nodded. "But we'll keep doing the best we can do because that's our only choice."

Gage couldn't argue with that.

THE NEXT MORNING, Gage woke up to a knock on his door. Easing out of bed and trying not to wake Lorelei, who was peacefully sleeping, he got up to take over the next shift on watch. He looked at Damon as he walked out. "Hey, anything going on?" he asked in a low voice.

Damon shook his head. "No, it's all clear, but ... I don't know. It feels off somehow."

Gage studied the look on his buddy's face. "Yeah, I've been feeling that way too."

"I presume we're waiting on an attack," Damon noted, with a shrug.

"And I hate that," Gage muttered. "If they want to attack, they should just come on and do it. I detest the waiting part."

Damon chuckled. "Well, if there is an attack, make sure you wake us up."

"Will do. Who set up the security here?" he asked. "I haven't had a chance to even look at it."

"Well, I set it up initially, but Wade added one of those hurricane alarms. Noisiest things ever."

"Oh, good," Gage replied. "In that case we should be fine. No sleeping through that."

"We should be," Damon agreed. "But you also know, like I do, that the *should-be*s don't necessarily always cut it in this business."

"That's for damn sure," Gage agreed. "I wish they did, but we can't ever let down our guard." He smiled at Damon. "Go get some sleep. You need some rest."

"Yeah, I will. Did you sleep okay?" Damon asked.

"I did finally." Gage nodded. "I'm frustrated, like everybody else, and second-guessing every decision, you know? But I finally just turned it all off and crashed, so I'll be fine for a few hours. Maybe I'll get something to eat." He rolled his eyes as he said it.

"Yeah, if those women left you anything, fly at it," Damon teased.

"I was planning on putting on some fresh coffee, if you want some," Gage offered.

"That sounds great, but I better take advantage of you being up and get myself a little sleep first."

"Go," Gage said. "It's five o'clock. I've got this. People will be up before long anyway."

And, with that, Damon turned and headed to his room.

Gage walked over to the coffeepot and got a pot started. While he waited for coffee, he moved over to where the computers were up and running data, and almost immediately he saw something that interested him. He sat down and studied the information in front of him, then started working his way through some of the other information available.

Somebody had set up a search for banking information associated with these guys who had hacked into their system a couple times recently. While the team had been sleeping, it had hit gold. There were payments made to a bank in Iran.

He studied the data for a long moment.

"Well, well, well," he muttered, "this is something positive. Now we just have to get somebody over there to deal with it." He didn't want to start pulling those kinds of strings, but it would really help a lot if they had some of Merk's men. Hopefully somebody from Levi's group could go over there, completely independent of them, so that nobody would know. Wondering about that, Gage sent Ice a message.

They all knew Ice to a certain extent. They were certainly getting to know her better and better over this mess. He got a response almost immediately, then realized that it was superlate for her and sent his reply. **Wow, that was quick. What on earth are you doing up? Everything okay?**

Her response came right away. **The baby is up.**

He smiled at that because it seemed an odd exchange, considering they both worked in black ops intelligence. If anybody was literally tracking their text messages, it would blow them apart to understand what they were saying. Talk about confusing, which was great, because anything that put them in better stead was good.

She quickly messaged again. **We can send a team over.**

He frowned, then replied, **I think somebody from here should go along.**

That's fine. Then came the next response. **Let's do joint.**

I'll wait until the team gets up. Then we'll contact you.

After receiving a thumbs-up emoji, he logged off. He hoped that Terk wouldn't get angry at him for stepping up on this, but, if they had somebody who could go, it was huge. He would go too, but his damn energy levels were the problem. For the first time he saw just how detrimental losing this type of skill was.

When it was full bore and working like a charm, he was hell on wheels. But injured, damaged, and not up to full speed, they were actually sitting ducks, with very little they could do about it. Considering that, he headed over, poured himself some coffee, and then sat down, going through a series of energy cycles to try to strengthen his field.

The biggest thing that Terk had ever gotten through to them was that, if your chips were down, the one thing you had to do was keep yourself controlled and all your energy pulled in tight, so you couldn't be found. If you were in trouble and had to help somebody else, that's where the source of that energy'll come from.

Gage didn't know what Terk was doing right now for his own energy but had noticed that Terk wasn't taking part in too much of the actual action. Gage also saw that Terk's energy was very low and very controlled. He wasn't sure why, but, when Terk was the first one up, Gage decided to ask.

Terk looked at him for a moment, then poured himself a cup of coffee. "The rest of the team," he murmured. "They're not dead. They're caught in stasis. So I'm trying to help them pull back to real life."

"Can you do that?" Gage asked, not totally surprised.

"Well, I've been trying to," Terk murmured. "That's how I got you here."

"I know. I totally know that, and I'm grateful. Believe me," Gage murmured, as he looked at his friend. "Are you telling me that you're doing that for everybody?"

Terk's lips quirked. "Yeah." Terk nodded. "That's why I'm not a whole lot of help in a lot of the other avenues."

"No," Gage countered, "you're doing even more than we could expect."

And then, knowing that Terk would find out pretty soon, Gage confessed, "Listen. I contacted Ice." Terk turned to face him. "I'll wait until everybody is up, but it looks like we've got some banking information that leads straight to Iran."

At that, Terk's face hardened. "Right, and you want Levi's help to check it out?"

"I think we just need faces nobody knows," Gage murmured. "We're about as visible as neon lights," he noted, "and the minute anybody makes the connection that we're not all dead, they'll wonder if anybody is."

"And we can't have that," Terk noted, staring off into space.

"The trouble is, it'll be damn hard to keep this charade up for much longer. With some of us back up, that'll be obvious really soon."

"Sure," Terk agreed, "but, at the same time, you and I both know we have to keep this up for as long as we can." He nodded, then sipped his coffee, and murmured, "Let me talk to them."

"Sure, I told Ice that we'd set up a meeting today," he added. "I was thinking maybe we could get one of our team to head over."

Terk just looked at him for a moment. "And, if we did that, it should be Calum because he speaks the language."

At that, Gage stopped and swore. "You know what? I wasn't even thinking that way, but we don't have the manpower anyway to send someone over there. I was thinking about trying to keep it on the quiet, but that won't help if we don't have anybody."

"Maybe we're better off to just send Levi's team."

"Maybe," Gage said cautiously.

"But what is it they'll go after? Levi's team won't have the same sensitivities or awareness or understand the same people over there that we did. They won't recognize the Iranian team, should any have survived. Levi's team can't do anything like that, since they don't have our experience in the field in Iran, much less the knowledge of the team we were sent to take down."

"Shit." Gage looked around. "I'll go then."

At that, Terk smiled. "Nope, you won't. We really need you here."

"I'm not doing anything here," Gage argued.

"Well, you will be soon."

At that, he froze and then slowly turned to look at Terk. "What does that mean?"

A sad smile came on Terk's face. "The attacks on Lorelei aren't over, and she'll need you before this is done."

"Terk, what does that mean?" Gage asked in growing alarm.

"It means the worst thing possible," he stated. "And you know that I never get any detailed answers. All I can tell you is what I see and what I feel."

"You got a time frame?"

"Yeah." Terk nodded. "And considering it's very soon, you may want to go crash for a few hours and spend it with her."

Gage sucked his breath back. "Seriously?"

There was absolutely no doubt in Terk's gaze. "Yes, seriously. You'll need everything you have," Terk noted, "so please don't exhaust yourself and stay at the ready." Gage headed to his room, as Terk added, "Yeah, and you'll need hooks."

"Shit! We are not supposed to do hooks."

"*Not do hooks* is one thing, but *not do hooks* when somebody is dying is a completely different thing. In this case you need to know in advance, and now you do," Terk murmured.

Such a sad look was on Terk's face that Gage felt his own heartstrings pulling hard. "Jesus, why her? She has already been through so much."

"I think the *why* has to do with the connection to us, and maybe somebody found out about her supposed secure line," he suggested. "The bottom line is, she's in trouble, and she doesn't have much longer."

"Can we do anything to stop it?" Gage asked, terrified of the answer.

"Stop it? No." Terk grimaced. "And you know that as well as I do. All we can do is try to minimize the fallout and to be as prepared and as ready as we can."

"Shit." Gage blew out a long slow breath. "Well, on that note, I'll be with Lorelei." He put down his cup and walked unsteadily toward the hallway door, where he turned back to his friend. "Anything else to add?"

"Not yet. Listen. I knew it when I saw her," Terk murmured. "That's one of the reasons I let her stay. You need to build that connection. You need to build it as hard and as strong as you can. At some point in time, you'll be the only reason she's still alive."

The two men stared at each other, and Gage could see the truth in Terk's gaze. Terk had experienced many premonitions in his life, and damn if they hadn't all come true. When Terk spoke, everybody stopped and listened. And right now Gage didn't want to hear this coming out of his friend's mouth. It was bad news the whole way. He nodded, headed toward the bedroom, but looked back at him once again. "Did you see an outcome?"

He gave him a sad smile. "You and I both know," Terk stated, "that outcomes are not set in stone. You do your part, and, if she does hers, we might get her through this. But, if you don't build that bond, there's no getting out of it." And, with that, Terk was gone.

CHAPTER 7

L ORELEI WOKE, FEELING a heat and a warmth wrapped around her that she hadn't expected. She tossed the covers off, groaning against the weight beside her.

"Easy," Gage murmured in her ear. "Just take it easy."

She opened her eyes. "Is it morning?" she asked, blurry-eyed.

"It is. I'm just coming in from a watch, and I'll spend a couple more hours here," he added, as he tugged her close.

"Hey, what's that got to do with spending a couple hours sleeping?" she asked in a teasing voice. But something was in the look on his face. She reached out, stroked his cheek. "What's the matter?" He didn't say anything and just held her close. Since that's exactly where she wanted him to be, she wouldn't argue. She nuzzled her chin against his neck and whispered, "Now if we only had privacy."

"We do," he said instantly. "Even when they do get up, they won't be worrying about us."

She smiled. "You don't mind if they know?"

"They already know." He laughed. "Don't think for a second that they don't."

She frowned. "It's back to that whole *I don't really know all of what you guys do* thing," she added.

"Maybe that's not a good thing," he admitted. "Just know that I really was planning on coming to see you, when this was all over with."

"Good," she said. "I thought we were on the same page there."

"We were. We are," he agreed, with a bright smile. "So don't worry about that at all."

"Well, that's good." She smiled. "Because, you know, this is starting to be a bit of a shit show."

"I disagree," he argued. "It *was* a shit show. But it's all much better now."

Rolling her eyes at him, she added, "Well, that's a load of BS."

"Nope. Not at all," he protested.

But she could tell something was still wrong. "Are you sure you're okay?" She looked directly at him. "You seem to be upset about something."

He swallowed, then nodded. "The only thing I'm upset about is the small amount of time that we've spent together. Like this." And, with that, he wrapped his arms around her and pulled her closer. She snuggled up against him, still wondering what he was trying to hide, and then decided it really didn't matter. If and when he wanted to tell her, he would, and, aside from that, she was delighted to cuddle up with him. She reached up, clasped his cheeks between her hands, and kissed him gently. "Well, we've wasted a ton of time, and I'm all for not wasting any more."

His lips quirked under her fingers in the half light, although the dawn was coming up pretty fast. He kissed her once and then twice, and she wrapped her arms around his neck and whispered, "Let's not waste another minute." She shifted her hips to press up tightly against his.

He looked at her for a long moment, and, once again, she was disturbed by the odd look in his eyes. Then he lowered his head, and he kissed her, like he really meant it. It was a kiss of passion and belonging, but more than that, it was almost desperation. She held him close, not knowing what was going on in his world. She wanted nothing more than to ease his pain, and she kissed him back with all her heart.

That kiss opened the floodgates between them. The promise of what if, the hopes that they had, and their dreams, all unspoken, because of the type of work they did. But, when that moment had opened up, giving them that possibility, that chance for something else, they'd been there, and they'd been more than willing to take it. And now she wasn't sure they even had a chance at something more any longer.

Maybe that was what was bothering him. Was it the attacks on her or his own attack? Maybe it was just that moment of realization that this could all end so quickly? Almost at the same time, it caught her in the back of her throat, as she realized just how damaged their whole world was and how wrong so many things in their world could go. She became acutely aware of how much they needed to fix and to heal.

When he raised his head the next time, he whispered, "Just look after yourself, would you?"

She immediately nodded. "Of course, and the same for you."

He grinned, then lowered his head, and this time there was absolutely no mistaking the power of the passion that drove them. She was stripped clean of all clothing within seconds. And she couldn't get his off fast enough.

Then he held her close and whispered, "This is for us." He finally smoothed his hands over her face, her breasts, and up and around her torso, then to her hips and across her flat belly, finally down to the smooth skin below. She was already in a state that wouldn't tolerate too much.

"I've wanted this for a very long time," she whispered, as she pulled him up tight. "So, no teasing." She could feel his smile against her lips.

"There's always time for teasing," he murmured.

She smiled, but then, when he started to lift his head up and away, she pulled him back down firmly. She kissed him with all the passion she had deep inside, until he shuddered in her arms and came back down, his lips hot, heavy, the passion driving deep into her belly.

By this time, her body was twisting, writhing beneath him, and, when he rose the next time, she wanted to protest, almost breathless with need. He eased himself into position, taking care of her injured leg and, without giving her any chance to say anything, he slipped inside. He stopped shuddering for a moment and then looked at her. With their gazes locked together, he slid all the way home.

She closed her eyes, feeling the incredible sense of rightness to his actions. The moment was powerful, far more powerful than she could ever have expected. But then he started to lift his hips and soon drove every thought from her heart and head, and it was just her body automatically responding to the pulsing pressure inside her. She started to move against him, gently at first and then heavier and harder, hotter and higher, until she was crying out with joy. He placed his lips over hers to seal in her cries, as the passion took hold and sent her flying.

When he followed a moment later and collapsed beside her, she knew a peace that she had never experienced before.

She lay here, encapsulated in his arms, held as if she were

the most wonderful thing in the world, and she knew that had something to do with whatever it was that was bothering him.

He leaned over and whispered, "You know I love you, right?"

She lifted her head, feeling the tears in her eyes, as she nodded. "I know. You always have."

He nodded, his smile a little wry as he looked at her. "And we waited, why?" he asked.

"Because something inside you was more worried about keeping me safe," she replied, "than about looking after yourself. And, as much as I agreed to a certain extent, this is not something I'm willing to forego anymore."

"Neither am I," he murmured. "Neither am I."

"And now can we just stay here?"

He shook his head. "No, we'll have a meeting soon." Gage yawned.

She frowned. "But you're exhausted."

"Nope, I'm not. I did get quite a bit of sleep," he murmured. "It's just seems like it was a while ago."

"That's because it *was* a while ago," she said, wiggling her eyebrows.

He grinned. "We're planning on sending a special recon team to Iran. I don't know which one of you three set up the banking traces for the people tracking us, hacking us," he explained, "but it leads to Iran."

She slowly leaned up on her elbow. "Does it?" she asked in excitement.

He nodded. "It does, indeed."

"Well, that's perfect," she replied. "Maybe we can at least lock down some of that BS."

"I'm hoping to lock it all down." Gage laughed.

She looked at him, "Well, you do realize, after our little session, I'll need a shower."

His eyes twinkling, he asked, "How do you feel about the two of us together in the shower?"

Her eyes widened. "Absolutely. Why waste water?" And, with that, she hobbled as quickly as her damaged body would allow, with him in hot pursuit.

LEVI WAS ALREADY seated when Ice sent through a message confirming the meeting. Everybody gathered at the dining table, waiting for her to connect.

As soon as her face filled the screen, Terk's team grinned at Levi, sitting right beside Ice, as she quickly studied everybody in front of them. Terk's whole team wasn't up and running yet. "How is everyone?" she asked quietly.

"We're fine," Tasha stated firmly.

Ice smiled. "And, if you're not, you will be, right?"

"Exactly." Tasha chuckled. "We're alive. We're well, and, so far, we're safe."

"And that's pretty good, considering what you've all been through," Levi said. "So what's this about Iran?"

Gage quickly ran through the results they had found on the banking trace, bringing everyone up to speed.

"Okay, so let us do a little bit more research," Ice suggested. "I've set a few of our people on it to see what we can come up with. Are you up for a joint task force to send to Iran, or you want us to go alone?"

"It would be better if you went with one of us," Terk replied quietly. "But the person you should go with isn't quite healed yet." At that, everybody turned to look at him.

"Seriously?" Gage asked. "Have you talked to Calum?"

Terk smiled. "Somewhat."

"Somewhat? What does that mean?"

"Let's just say he's surfacing. But, like you, he'll be a little while." Terk hesitated and then murmured, "Let's say a bit weakened."

"Damn it," Gage said, "but, at the same time, I'm thrilled he's making progress."

Tasha stared at Terk in delight. "Really? Will one more of the team return to us?"

"More than one," Terk replied, "but, for the moment, it's all about them getting their strength back." Terk paused. "That's the reason for the coma, to protect them. Then once they reach a certain healing point, the coma gradually recedes, and they come back out of it again."

"In spite of you keeping them down too, I presume," Tasha added.

Terk looked at her in surprise, and a reluctant grin popped out, as he nodded. "Yes, you could say that."

"Did you think we don't know that you've been trying to keep them all alive, even though you're suffering yourself in a big way?" she noted, with an eye roll.

"I've got to do what I've got to do for my friends," he murmured.

"And we get that," she said. "We really do. But, at the same time, it's pretty darn hard to watch you burn through your energy and not give a damn."

At that, Merk popped into the chat. "Hey, I'm here too," he added. "Nobody better be making any plans without me."

"Not possible," Levi added in a wry tone. "You're like a bad penny. You pop up everywhere."

"That's the job." Merk grinned at his old friend. "Iran though, that sounds rough."

"It can be, so I'm not too sure who I'd send. Plus we need a plan before anybody goes," Ice stated firmly. "No mission goes forward without a clear objective."

"We're still looking for any living members of this bloody team that we took down," Terk said. "Look into that for me, will you?"

"Give me the details on the mission," she noted. "This is the one where you supposedly took down everybody involved. Is that it?"

He nodded. "Yeah, and we honestly thought we had everyone."

"And you're thinking that's who is behind this?"

"I honestly don't know, Ice. What I can tell you is that we also had a suspicion or intel that said we had somebody with software who was doing something similar."

"It could be that the US government was working on that over in Iran too," Levi murmured.

"Maybe. I don't know who's doing what anymore," Terk admitted. "All I can tell you is that assholes of every kind are everywhere, and, just when I think we get clear of one, there's another."

At that, Levi burst out laughing. "And that's the honest-to-God truth, no matter where we are," Levi agreed, "because these assholes are all over—not just in Iran. They're in the US. They're in England. They're on all soils," he noted. "It's like a hydra. As soon as we cut off one head, another dozen pop up."

"Right." Terk gave a shake of his head. "It's BS, all of it."

"Well, for what it's worth, I really feel like we should

delay the mission," Gage suggested quietly, "until we see if we can put our best guy in the job for backup."

"Calum speaks Farsi far more fluently than the rest of us and would definitely be our best choice to do this trip," Terk replied. "If it's not possible, it's not, but, if there is a chance at sending him, it would be worth waiting for."

"I get it," Ice agreed. "Listen. We can do some reconnaissance, if you want, but maybe we're better off to plan this for next week." She looked over at Damon. "Damon, you're worried about something. What is it?"

And her tone was so blunt that, although he wanted to take offense, it was pretty damn hard to. Damon glanced over at Terk, then frowned. "I just think it's the circumstances."

She glared at him, obviously hearing him trying to push it off, signaling he wouldn't get engaged in that conversation. Finally she let it go. "Terk, I'll need to talk with you before any new scenarios happen anyway."

"Problems?" he asked.

She hesitated. "Not so much problems but Celia is waking a bit."

He froze, then looked at her and asked, "That's a good thing, isn't it?"

"It is," she said quietly. "I just don't know what information she'll have for us."

"Well, hopefully she'll have information that's helpful," he said bluntly, "but I highly suspect she doesn't know anything."

"And I suspect you're right about that," she agreed. "In that case, what is it you want us to do?"

He hesitated. "Can you just keep her safe, keep her out of this, don't let her know what's going on?" he asked.

She tilted her head. "What will that do?"

"Hopefully," he replied, "it will let her heal without getting involved."

"What if she knows something?"

He winced and stared off in the distance. "I don't know," He shook his head, as if at a loss for an answer. "She obviously has something to say," he murmured. "I mean, she didn't get hooked up to that C-4 for nothing. I just don't know what she can tolerate amid all this."

"We never do," Ice added gently, "until it happens, and then we find out. Let me see what state she's in mentally and physically, and we'll go from there."

Terk nodded slowly. "And if she needs to be under for a little bit longer …"

She looked at him, smiled. "Terk, you can't put it off forever," she said gently. "When she's ready, I'll bring her back out, and we'll talk." And, with that, everybody had to be satisfied, because honestly arguing with Ice just didn't work. She had a lot going on, and she always put herself out there to ensure what needed to be done was taken care of. But she also was very direct and efficient and expected the same in return. She ended the call soon afterward.

Gage looked over to see Lorelei sitting at the table, working away on a plate of French toast. He shook his head.

"Yeah, don't even say anything," she retorted. "That's the smart way to get out of this."

"I don't know what to say," he replied, with laughter in his voice.

"Hey, I'm hungry," she noted, "and that's a good thing, right? It means that I'm healing."

"It does, indeed." Terk smiled. "You eat as much as you want."

"Glad to hear that." She looked around at the others. "Anybody else want some? I made plenty while your meeting had been on. It's warming in the oven."

"Damn, yes," Gage replied. "Absolutely."

She smiled, as the group happily converged for breakfast.

CHAPTER 8

E ACH MEMBER OF Terk's team was given their particular job to do, whether feeding more energy to Calum to bring him out of the coma, well enough to handle the planned Iran op, or to secure their warehouse from an impending attack or ... something else.

Lorelei continued to watch Damon's demeanor over the next few hours as they executed plans. Something was off, and she didn't know what it was, but she certainly wasn't in a position to say anything because she didn't know Damon as well as she would like to. It was always possible that she was reading something wrong. But, when she caught Tasha looking at him with a puzzled expression too, Lorelei realized it wasn't just her. Finally she couldn't handle it anymore and spoke up. "You need to explain what's going on, Damon," she stated bluntly.

He looked at her in surprise. "What's the matter?"

"Something is off with you," Lorelei stated. "You're acting all weird."

He stared at her, raising his eyebrows, and then laughed. "I don't think so," he muttered.

"Well, I do," she argued. "Everybody else is looking at you strangely too, if you hadn't noticed." He checked around the room. The men seemed to want to disappear, but Sophia and Tasha were both staring at Damon expectantly.

He shrugged. "Hey, I'm just doing my job." He held up both hands. "Nothing wrong with that." And since he wouldn't discuss it, there wasn't a whole lot Lorelei could do about it. But she didn't like it, not one bit, and the fact that he was trying to hide *whatever* just made her that much more suspicious. She sighed, then settled back. "Fine—well, it's not fine—but, when you're ready to talk, remember that I'm right here."

Damon gave her a brilliant smile. "I know, and I really appreciate that."

With that, she had to be satisfied and returned to her own work. She watched and waited as everybody else resumed their tasks. She didn't know what exactly the overall plan was, but it had something to do with getting one of their team back up and running. She watched and listened, but not a whole lot of it made any sense.

Finally she couldn't stand it anymore. "I get that this team member is somebody you're trying to bring back into the fold," she noted, "but I'm really not understanding what the problem is."

At that, they stopped, looked at her and at each other, and then just shrugged.

She felt her temper starting to rise. "Come on," she stated sharply. "Like it or not, I'm here, and, while I don't know everything that goes on, I've been working with this team for a long time. Obviously I'm not privy to everything, but, in this circumstance, it would be awfully nice if I wasn't shut out."

"Okay," Gage said quietly. "Clearly we need to answer your questions, so you better understand what we do."

"I know that you guys were doing some remote-viewing work," she noted, "similar to a cold-war program."

He nodded. "That's quite true, and we've had mixed results with it."

"Of course," she huffed. "That's not exactly technology you can just tweak as you want."

"No, it isn't," Gage agreed. He looked at her screen, then frowned. "How is your work going?"

"Well, I still have access, and, so far, whoever that poor woman is in the morgue hasn't been on the news, and nobody has mentioned anything to me."

He nodded.

"You think she was killed in my stead, right?"

"That's my presumption, yes," Gage agreed. "It makes the most sense."

"Right. I get it," she acknowledged, "and you're trying to stop them from finding out that the wrong person is dead."

"Chances are good already," he added, "that, when you tried to log in and couldn't, then demanded that you be given access again, somebody already found out."

She winced. "Right, so maybe it wasn't the time to be proactive."

He shrugged. "They would have found out soon enough anyway. It's just a matter of whether they have anybody left to do the job."

"But an assassin was already after me, right?"

"Well, that's what we're thinking. Potentially he did the second hit and run, killing the woman in the morgue. By that theory they found out right away that it was the wrong person, and now the hitman is after you."

She winced at that. "So we don't know if it's the guy I saw in my hotel or who could be the separate hitman we were told about—Bingo—by one of the two park shooters,

Joachim." She slumped in her chair. "Always great to know that you're worth killing," she said caustically. "Wouldn't it have been nice of them to have found out if I'd done something to actually deserve it?"

"In their world," Gage explained, "you don't have to do anything to deserve it or not. The fact that you still exist, when you aren't supposed to, means something went wrong."

She nodded. "I get it. I get it. I'm not supposed to exist. *Great.* Thanks. Did anybody think about that poor woman and her family?"

"I'm sure all of us have," Gage noted. "But it still doesn't change the fact that, where we're at right now, we can't do a whole lot about it yet."

"Is there anything else I can do?"

"Nope." Gage shook his head. "Heal. ... That would be the best thing."

She rolled her eyes at that. "I'm starting to feel like a puppy dog here."

He burst out laughing, then leaned over and kissed her on the cheek. "Never, although you'd make a damn cute one."

At that, the others all choked with laughter.

He rolled his eyes. "It's very different not having any privacy."

"Yep," Damon agreed, with a smile. "Listen. We need to pick up supplies that Levi has sent over."

"I'll go," Gage murmured. He hopped to his feet, then looked around and asked, "Anybody else?"

Terk spoke up. "Damon and I'll come."

Gage frowned, looked at his friend. "You're not in very good shape." But he got a flat stare in return. "Fine." Gage raised his palms. "But only if you think it's better that you don't stay here and guard everybody else," he argued, with a tilt of his head toward Lorelei.

Terk shook his head. "Nope, I need to come with you." And that definitive tone to his voice meant there was a damn good reason, and nobody could talk Terk out of it.

"Someday I hope to get good enough to make those decisions like you do," Gage replied.

"Someday I hope somebody around here will give me a little bit more explanation as to why Terk gets to say things like that, and everybody just falls into line," Lorelei added.

"I'll share a little bit with you, when they're gone," Tasha noted, as she looked over at Terk and Gage. "With your permission of course." They both nodded.

"It's time," Terk said.

"Thank you for that," Lorelei murmured.

Terk nodded, then smiled. "You may not thank us afterward." And, with that, he headed to the doorway. "It will be," he stopped, his head tilted to the side, "a couple hours."

At that, even Gage turned and looked at him. "Really?" he asked, and Terk nodded again.

"Yeah, I don't think it'll go as smoothly as we thought it would." With that, he was gone, Damon behind him.

Immediately Gage felt the protest rising in the back of his throat, but there was absolutely no point in arguing with Terk. A decree had been made, and, for whatever reason, they would still go.

He looked over at the others. Seeing the look of worry on Lorelei's face, he smiled at her and added, "Don't worry. I'm even safer having Terk with me." And, with that, he bolted after his friends. He heard her voice as he moved away.

"Okay, now somebody needs to give me a damn explanation."

Gage hoped they would go easy on her because some things were a whole lot easier to understand than others. When he got into the vehicle with Terk and Damon, and they pulled out of the parking lot, Gage asked Terk, "Do you think that's wise?"

"What?" he asked bluntly.

"Letting her know what's going on."

"How do you expect to keep her out of it?" he murmured. "The minute everybody opened their hearts and souls to relationships," he explained, "the game changed."

Damon silently nodded in the back seat.

"Ouch." Then Gage thought about it and finally nodded too. "I guess it did at that. So now what?"

"So *now what* is that we have more people to keep safe," Terk stated, "something that we always held back from doing in order to keep ourselves separate and above all this. I guess, at this point in time, with the sudden breakup with the government and all that bureaucratic mess before we were attacked, everybody had made some personal plans, and things changed," he noted simply.

"You made plans too."

"*Huh?* You're right. I did. I told you that."

"I know," he agreed. "I'm just wondering how life played out and blew up all our plans."

"I don't know," Terk replied. "Sometimes I think life is just one big damn game, and we don't know the rules. I think that a lot, actually," he muttered. "It'd be nice if we did have some heads-up notice as to how to play things, but it never seems to work that way."

"No, it sure doesn't," Gage murmured.

They headed out, following the GPS to the bus depot, where they loaded up one box, and then over to FedEx, where they loaded up two other packages. Gage looked at Terk, as he hopped back into the truck. "Is that it?"

"Yeah, except for groceries."

He stopped, looked at him with a frown. "We just got—"

"Every time we come out, it's better to pick up something."

"Good Lord." Gage shook his head. "It's those women, who seem to outeat us."

Damon chuckled.

"I know, right?" Gage agreed. "But will you fund this indefinitely, Terk? I can chip in. God knows Lorelei's been putting a hurt on the groceries."

"Jesus, don't do that. Then I'll have to pay for Tasha," Damon added, and they all shared a good laugh.

"Yeah, don't worry about it, Gage," Terk replied. "We've got the money from the government's bank account they had all set up for us."

Gage stared at Terk. "Jeez, I didn't know that."

"Yeah, I can't keep track of who I've told about what, with you guys coming back on one at a time. I secured the money right away, not sure what was going on with the government, and I haven't worried much about it," Terk said, "at least until we know who's trying to kill us. And, for now, I don't feel guilty about taking that money at all."

"And they don't know?"

"They don't have any access," Terk said, with half a smile. "I do, and that's it."

"Well, you might want to share that access with somebody, just in case."

"I agree. We've got to keep building redundancy into

everything we do," Terk agreed.

"That is a good idea," Damon added.

"And is there enough to cover everything we need for a while?" Gage asked.

"Everything we need and to set up a startup, if we want."

Gage looked over at him and nodded. "We had a bit of discussion about that, when I was out with Wade the other day."

"That's to be expected," Terk replied. "Everybody is trying to redefine what we're doing right now," he murmured.

"And what are we doing?" Gage asked. "Seems to be an exercise in frustration. It would be nice if we had some idea of what was really going on."

"Nobody can make plans until this is over," Terk noted. "I don't even know how many of us will still be standing."

"Yet we're bringing more of the guys back online, right?"

"Yes." He nodded. "We have to."

"Yeah," Damon chimed in. "Not so long ago, it was just the two of us. Having you and Wade back, plus the women, has helped more than you can even imagine."

Gage winced at that. "I don't even want to think about it. But, Terk, do you ever worry that you're wrong?"

"All the time," he murmured, "but I didn't train all you guys to follow me blindly." He paused. "You have senses. You have your own abilities. You should be using them, to the extent that you're able."

"Oh, I am," Gage confirmed. "But what I can do and what you can do—there is no comparison." He shook his head. "You can do everything I can do, plus more. You've told me that before." His voice was tight with frustration.

"I think this scenario has the ability to show you just what you can do," Terk murmured. "I just hope it doesn't kill you in the process."

"Good God," Gage said. "It's never comfortable hearing you discuss things like that."

"Of course not," he murmured. "Why would it be? The trouble is, none of this is comfortable, but, most of the time, you'll grow through the worst-case scenarios."

"I get it," Gage replied, "but all we're doing at the moment is hiding."

Terk looked over at him, his lips twitching. "I know, and there's a good reason for it."

Gage sighed. "What's the reason?"

"We're waiting for the rest of the team to come on board."

"Ah, well, that still makes it pretty shitty in the long run," he replied.

"It does, and it doesn't, but I can't tell you anything other than that," he murmured. "As you know, some things just have to happen the right way."

"Yeah, I hear you. It's always that way, isn't it?"

"It is, and we can never rush it," Terk stated. "Whether we want to or not."

And, with that, Gage had to be satisfied, and Damon tried to distract him with examples of prior cases, where waiting had worked in their favor.

AFTER STOPPING BY the grocers, when they were about six blocks away from the compound, Terk's phone buzzed with a text message. He pushed a button on his cell. "Shit."

"What is it?" Damon asked.

"It says, *Stay away. Under attack.*" Damon hit the brakes

immediately and looked at Terk. "And they expect us to stay away?"

"It's from Tasha." Terk immediately hit the Call button on his phone, then hit Speaker.

When she answered, she cried out, "Don't come home. We don't know what's going on, but people are down, and I'm not sure what's doing it."

"No way in hell," Gage yelled into Terk's phone, "that we'll leave you guys alone like that."

"Listen. I think that, whatever it is, is a psychic attack or something," Tasha explained. "I don't know what the hell, but maybe—I don't know." Her voice broke off, and the guys heard the tremendous worry in it.

"I hate to ask, but how is Lorelei?" Gage asked.

"She was working here and then she went to lie down. I presume she still is."

"Right," Damon said, nodding at Terk, "but we won't leave you alone, so expect us to be coming in, one way or another. But we'll do a full reconnaissance first."

She groaned. "I want you here. Believe me, but I don't want anybody else to go down. We need somebody out there to try to save us."

"We got it." Terk hung up.

Gage looked over at Terk to see his eyes closed, but his fingers were clenched together in a fist. "If you need my energy, go ahead." At that, Gage felt a probe coming his way. He opened up his senses and let Terk lock on. They were always much stronger together.

Gage could see a little bit of what Terk was doing, but it would require more of Terk's energy to show Gage and Damon more. The three of them were safe for the moment on the side of the road and were only a couple blocks away, but Gage knew if anybody came by and saw how they were sitting here, looking so odd, they'd likely get the cops called on them. He tried to appear as normal as he could, then brought up his phone. It took great effort because of the link to Terk, but he managed to send a text message to Lorelei. **You there?**

Yes.

Apparently the compound is under attack.

Weird. *Hmm*, it's hard to move, … no strength.

Mechanical? He didn't know what else to ask her. **Go into the bathroom and hide in the bathtub. Lie down flush, so there's less interference.** He waited for a response, and, when it came, it was a good few minutes later.

In bathtub, slightly better.

He nodded. "It could be mechanical," he told Terk.

"It could be," he muttered, his voice hoarse and thick. "But somebody is running it."

"Can you track it?"

"I don't know about tracking it." Terk shook his head. "I think it's close by. It could also be human, I suppose," he muttered to himself.

"Same diff," Damon noted.

"It could also be both," Terk offered. "They've been testing psychic energy machines, and this is a great way to do it." With that, he said, "I'm heading in." Terk broke the connection to Gage, looked at Damon. "We both are. Gage, come with me. Damon, you take the perimeter, in case we go down."

Damon didn't like it but was accustomed to taking orders without argument.

They all hopped out, locked up the vehicle, and raced down a couple blocks, following the strange hum. Their temporary compound was a huge warehouse that took up one block. Gage hadn't surveyed the whole footprint of it. He gathered it was once one gigantic warehouse that had been broken up into several smaller ones or the various ones were now all one warehouse.

Regardless, in case of an emergency, they had an alternate window entrance at the rear of this block. They could hide out here in this section, if needed, or, in a pinch, could access their inhabited portion. They came in on the farthest side of the complex, where the warehouse had no ground-floor windows. Only a few windows were on the second floor at this end, and, moving a nearby dumpster, they gained entrance to the designated window that they had left deliberately unlocked and accessible just to them. If you knew where the window was, it was easy to enter but difficult to find if you had no foreknowledge.

Once inside the building, Gage fell to his knees. Outside, he had heard the hum, but, inside, Jesus, it was incredible.

Terk fell to his knees beside him.

They looked at each other, their gazes both pain-filled, and Terk mouthed, "I'll have to get out," and he immediately bolted for the window behind him.

Gage stood and set up the blockades that he needed. Terk was much more sensitive and was utilizing his energy on multiple pathways, so this would have been agonizing for him. For Gage himself, well, he would do what he could to knock this interference down to something more manageable.

It took a good couple minutes for him to put up the blocks, essentially shoring up the debilitating high-pitched noise, so it wouldn't keep them all down. At the last moment, he severed the connection between Terk and himself, leaving Terk without Gage's energy. *Sorry.*

Still hearing that heavy dull motion of machinery, he headed toward the right side of the building. He snuck deeper inside, checking the hallways and doors as he went.

They—or it—had to be here somewhere. He could sense the energy gaining in power when he went to the left. He hesitated, because the safety of his friends was to the right, but he had to deal with this problem on the left. He had to get to whoever or whatever this threat was in order to save everybody else. He slid closer and closer, pulling out the small ankle revolver he kept on him. It was typically the only thing he carried when he was traveling. He also had a switchblade in his pocket.

With both out and accessible, he came up to a closed door, put an ear against it, and tried to listen. It sounded empty. He pushed it open and immediately stepped in, with his gun drawn. But no one and nothing was here.

He stepped out again and did the same across the hall. As he looked down the hallway, he noted at least a dozen more doorways. Swearing because it was just him and realizing it was too easy for him to lose focus with that toned-down but pulsing racket going on in the background, Gage put up a few more bricks in the blockade to try to shore it up, and then headed down to another door and then another.

At the third door in, he stopped because he heard something. He gently turned the knob, then pushed it open and stepped inside. "Hands up," he snapped. What he saw in front of him made his heart freeze—a little boy and a young woman. She stared at him, tears in her eyes, clutching the child close against her chest. Gage holstered his gun and put away the knife and took a deep breath and motioned at her. "Are you a prisoner here?"

She tilted her head, and he repeated the question in French this time. She immediately nodded, telling him that they'd been kidnapped at home and brought here.

When he asked if she knew why, an odd look came to her face, and he knew she was about to lie. He stopped her with a hand motion. "We don't have time for lies. You tell me the truth."

She whispered, "I have," and then, with a deep breath, she continued. "I have some abilities, they think."

He nodded. "And are you using them right now?"

"No choice," she stated. "They're tapped in."

His eyebrows shot up at that. "That's not good. Can you break it?"

She shook her head. "Something's in my neck," she whispered, still holding the kid, who was bawling in her arms.

Gage immediately stepped forward and tilted her head down. "Shit." He pulled the switchblade from his pocket. "This will hurt." She tensed up, and he sliced the skin, feeling her jolt. And there, indeed, was a small device, a tracker or a transmitter. He popped it free, dropped it to the ground, then immediately crushed it with his foot.

She sank back, and he could see the relief throughout her whole body.

"Give your nerves a few moments to not jangle anymore," he told her.

She looked up. "I will. I will. Thank God," she murmured. "I need to get out of here."

"What you need to do is stay safe," he stated, "and that means staying here."

She shook her head. "But they'll be back. They'll know that the device's gone, and they'll be back."

"Good. How about I wait here with you?"

She looked at him hopefully. "How about you wait and let me go instead?"

He considered that and looked down at the little boy. Frowning, he asked, "Who is this little guy?"

She hesitated.

"He looks familiar," he stated bluntly.

"His name is Calum." She looked up at Gage, her eyes huge, then whispered, "He's named after his father."

At that, Gage felt like he took a heavy punch to the gut.

"Jesus, you know him?" she asked.

"I'm on his team."

She brightened considerably. "We came looking for him," she cried out. "He's here somewhere. I know it."

"How do you know that?" Again she flushed. "Your abilities?"

She nodded. "I just know that he's within a few miles."

"And he's surfacing"—Gage nodded—"but he's been injured and not at full strength. He's not even conscious yet."

"He is though. I heard his voice," she said eagerly. "I need to get to him. He needs to know that we're safe."

He stared at her in shock. "He knows about the kid?"

She nodded slowly. "Yes, we're the forgotten family," she muttered. "But he knows about us, and he sends us money every month."

He shook his head. "Wow, the things you don't know about your team."

"He walked away because it was too dangerous for us," she explained. "I hated him for it. I hated him so much for robbing us of his presence." She looked around the room, her tears now flowing in earnest. "But he was right," she said brokenly. "He was right."

Gage studied the boy and saw the clear resemblance to his father. "In that case, I'll stay here with you, until it's safe, then you'll stay with me," he murmured.

She shook her head. "No, I have family too, and they'll be worried."

"We'll deal with all that later but first things first. We have to get you back to safety, and that isn't here." At that, he heard something down the hallway and immediately held a finger to his lips.

Her gaze widened, and she looked down at the kid and tried to tell him to shush, but he wasn't having any of it. The little boy was wailing hard.

Just then the door opened, and Gage had barely enough time to step behind it.

"Shut that kid up," the new arrival snapped, "or I'll do it for you." And, sure enough, a handgun came up in a threatening motion.

Since the man was alone, Gage didn't hesitate. He grabbed the handgun, turned it to the ground, and crushed the fingers holding it, even as he turned and flipped the gunman, his heel catching the other man in the groin. Then Gage completed his turn, giving him a hard smack with his elbow, knocking him to the ground, where he immediately dropped to his knees. Gage followed with a hard right to the jaw. And, just like that, the gunman was out cold.

Gage immediately closed the door, walked back over to the man and pulled off his shoes and socks, using the socks to tie his hands behind him. Then he took off his belt and tied up his feet. He looked over at the frightened woman. "Is this one of the men who kidnapped you?"

She nodded. "My God, what did you do?"

"The same thing Calum would have done, if he were here," he reassured her.

She took a deep breath. "I didn't really understand. I owe him such an apology."

"Yeah, you also owe him some understanding. He really did look after you and the child first, and I'm sure it killed him to do it."

"I get it," she whispered. "I just love him so much, and it was so hard to watch him walk away."

He nodded. "I get that too, but, at the moment, what we'll do is figure out how to get you out of here. I also need to know what they're doing and then stop it." At that, he felt a transmission in his head. "Terk is here," Gage announced.

She looked at him. "Terk? That's Calum's boss."

He nodded. "He is. Does he know about you?"

She shrugged. "He contacted me and told me when Calum was injured."

"Of course he did," Gage muttered. Was there ever anything in Terk's world that happened without him knowing about it? Just then came a slight tap on the door. Gage immediately headed behind the door but quickly realized it was Terk. He pulled open the door, still holding the gun at the ready, just in case. Terk stepped inside, took one look at Gage, saw the guy on the floor and the woman with the crying child in her arms.

"Good. Once I realized we had a different energy in here," Terk explained, "I had to come back inside."

"Apparently you know who this is?" Gage asked Terk.

He looked over at the woman and smiled. "Mariana, how are you?"

"Now that I'm free, I'm okay." She hopped up, and, carrying the child awkwardly, she walked over toward him. "There were three others," she added quietly. "And they have some sort of machine."

At that, Gage took over the story. "I also took out a transmitter that they had put into her neck."

At that, Terk's face turned grim. "They'll pay for that. We'll get her into the compound and keep her safe. I've called out for the others."

"The others?" Gage asked.

"When you knocked off the noisemaker transmitter," Terk explained, "I got Wade awake. He's on his way. And, so far, Damon isn't seeing anything outside."

"Well, at least one more will help," Gage murmured.

"They'll all help," Terk corrected. "It's just a matter of timing."

"We need to stop these guys," Gage snapped. "We can't have them attacking civilians and planting devices in them."

"I get it." Just then came a buzz on Terk's phone. He smiled. "That's Wade. He's right outside."

Gage looked over at Mariana. "I'll take you to a window, and we'll have to go through it and drop to the ground."

She took a deep breath. "Fine, if it gets me outside."

"Not only outside," Gage corrected, "but we'll take you where you'll see the rest of Calum's team."

She looked at him, her gaze hard. "I want to go to Calum."

"You won't need to," Terk noted. "Against my best advice, Calum is trying to get to you."

Her eyes lit up. "Okay, that's a good thing then," she murmured.

"Listen, Mariana. He's still not functioning properly,

and he doesn't have all his senses about him," he tried to warn her. "But he heard your cry for help."

She flushed and whispered, "Yes, I didn't think about that."

"I know." Terk nodded. "And, in this case, it's fine. Obviously we have to get you and your boy safe."

And, with that, they disappeared down the hallway. Gage came behind them, keeping watch to make sure nobody else attacked them. At the window, Gage saw Wade down below, climbing onto the dumpster. The child was passed to him, and he got them both safely to the ground. Then Mariana awkwardly moved out through the window, with Terk's help, and dropped to the dumpster by herself, then jumped to the ground.

That done, Terk joined Gage once more. "I'll sweep through the back of this warehouse and see what else I can come up with. You go through the front of it."

"Got it," Gage nodded. And knowing that the woman and her child were safe, he headed deeper inside. The whole thing was something that still blew him away. Everybody seemed to have a personal life that they hadn't necessarily shared with anybody else on the team, yet Terk appeared to know about almost all of them.

CHAPTER 9

LORELEI HUDDLED IN the bathtub; some of the horren-
dous hum, which had been a driving buzz into her
brain, eased back slightly. With her phone, she quickly
texted Tasha in the other room. **Are you okay? I'm hiding
in the bathtub.**

Good. Stay there. The men are coming back.

Is that wise?

Maybe not but we need help.

Got it. Can I do anything?

**Stay there and out of the way. I don't know where
the attack is coming from, so I can't do anything except
try to keep some semblance of control and keep track of
where everybody is.**

Got it. And then she thought about the others. **Is Sophia okay? And Wade?**

**She's out cold but seems unhurt. I think it's the de-
bilitating noise level.**

**Yes, it would be. I could try to get her and bring her
in here?**

**No, just stay where you are. She's out cold and not
suffering right now, so let's not risk it.**

"She'll have a hell of a headache when she wakes up
though," Lorelei muttered to herself, as she put down her
phone.

Although Lorelei was somewhat out of danger, she

knew, sure as hell, that if she got out and tried to do anything to help, it would not work out so well. But she had to offer because she didn't want to see anybody else hurting.

As she lay here, she wondered if she could do anything else, and she quickly texted an update to Gage. But she warned him that it was bad news. The response that came back surprised her. Wade had left and apparently was on his way here. She wanted to scream at him to stop, only to realize that he had left to go get somebody and was now returning.

At that point, some of the humming sensation dimmed ever-so-slightly yet again. She frowned, wondering what that was. But, as she continued to lay here, her senses attuned to something, almost like she heard something. She had never explored the other rooms in this place, now wondering just what all could be inside them.

What were the chances that somebody had come into their headquarters when they weren't aware of it? She didn't know how that would be, but obviously something like that had happened, and even now the intruders were moving from room to room, getting closer and closer. Whatever they were doing involved that noisemaker. It was almost like some sensory deprivation noise. She thought, if she were a dog, she'd be howling at the top of her lungs.

Hell, she wanted to do it anyway. She crouched lower and lower, wondering if she could put a towel over her head. And then suddenly the door to her bedroom opened.

She strained her ears, trying to hear who was coming, and stared at the connecting bathroom door in fear. She quickly texted Gage that her bedroom door had opened. His only response was telling her to stay there, to stay down, and to stay quiet.

"Yeah, I figured out that part," she muttered to herself. But that didn't help much if this went south quickly.

Suddenly the bathroom door burst open. She lay as flat as she could, and the bathtub was just ever-so-slightly around the corner. Then she heard a laugh, and she knew that she'd been found. She opened her eyes to find a man standing in front of her, holding a gun in one hand and something else in his other.

He smiled at her. "Ah, exactly who I was looking for."

Her eyebrows popped up. "What?" she squeaked out. He shut off the thing in his hand for a moment, and she suddenly heard better.

"The missing analyst." He chuckled. "You weren't supposed to survive this long. Nice job."

She stared at him in horror, realizing that all of this was about her. All this nastiness was about somebody trying to get at her. "Why are you trying to kill me?" she cried out. "I didn't do anything to you."

"Maybe not, but you did it to somebody," he replied carelessly. "And I don't want to listen to any sob stories. I'm really not in the mood. You've been hard to find, but I've got you now."

"You think so?" she asked quietly.

"Oh, I know so." He raised the gun.

She could do absolutely nothing. She was too far away to do anything, and then he turned the noisemaker back on, she realized immediately that her movements were impacted, as she tried to shift in the bathtub. Her efforts to sit up and to get out were limited now because of the noisemaker. Worse than that, it would also keep anybody else from reacting to whatever it was he planned to do to her. He grabbed her arm, then laid her back down.

"Stay there." Then he put the gun against her temple but suddenly tilted his head, as if listening. She realized somebody else was out there. Holding her breath, hoping against hope that it was true, she pleaded with the man with her eyes, but he wasn't having any of it.

Suddenly a sound came from behind him. He immediately pivoted, looking toward the door and headed out of the bathroom. He also did something with the noisemaker, increasing the volume of the sound.

She gasped, and grabbing a towel hanging off the tub, wrapped it around her head, holding it pressed tightly against her ears. That muffled it a little bit. Now she was worried about whoever was behind the door.

She moved forward until she was sitting up, then managed to slip from the bathtub, falling on her good side. There was no place for her to go, but, damn it, she wanted to get the hell out of here. Other people were here, who needed to be protected too. She crawled her way to the bedroom and saw no sign of her gunman. He obviously thought she was no threat, and, although he was right, it also pissed her off in a way.

She made it to the bed and pulled herself up, so that she was standing, although a little on the wobbly side. Then she walked to the doorway, and there she stopped because she heard no human sounds anywhere, except for the noisemaker. She wrote a quick text but held off sending it, afraid to get Gage caught by the noise. She didn't want to do anything to tip off anyone as to where Gage was.

She headed in the opposite direction of the main room, moving slowly but surely toward the hallway and whatever was down there. She should have asked him more about this warehouse. It was a huge building from the outside, but she really didn't know what went on inside all of it. She kept going, and, as she did, the noise got a little bit easier to handle.

With some of that under control, she picked up her pace and started to run as far away as she could with her bad leg. They were after her, after all, so maybe she could draw them away and save somebody. She hoped the others wouldn't think she was just trying to save herself because that wasn't true at all.

She didn't know what else she was supposed to do to help, when it was so hard to even function back there when in the range of the noisemaker. If there was a way to stop the noisemaker, that would be perfect, but unfortunately it seemed to be something he had control of in his hand. Looking down at the text in her phone, she brought the message back up and quickly hit Send, hoping that she hadn't killed Gage.

When she got a response back a few minutes later, she wrote back, **I'm down the hallway, but he headed toward you guys.**

Keep going. Get out if you can.

She sent back another message. **I don't want to leave everyone.**

Don't worry. We've got this.

And, with that, she had to trust him, so she turned and bolted, looking for an exit, running as fast as she could. She got another text.

Run. They're after you. Run.

She bolted as hard and as fast as she could. When she hit the exit on the other side, she burst through it without a thought. And fell right into the waiting arms, … unfortunately not the right ones.

GAGE HAD NO clue whether Lorelei had managed to get out or not. He was still hunting the one using the handheld device controlling the horrible noise. He found him in the main room, wandering around, looking carefully at all the materials that they had. "We don't like uninvited visitors."

The guy immediately froze.

"Hands up," Gage ordered. A quick glance told him that Tasha was motionless on the floor, and Sophia was not here. His heart hardened. "And shut off that damn thing."

"Sure, no problem," the guy replied.

Gage knew instinctively that he'd turn it up. Gage quickly threw up blocks, racing forward.

The guy just smiled and turned it higher and higher and higher.

Gage reached out in his mind, and Terk was instantly there with more blocks, throwing them up in front of him. By the time he reached the intruder, who was now laughing hysterically, Gage's right fist connected with the man's jaw, and down he went. Gage stared at him blindly on the floor, as he moved over to the transmitter and stomped on it. It instantly stopped, and all the noise came to a grinding halt. The peace, the silence, was deafening.

Still, with his wits about him, he held his gun on the intruder. "Drop the gun." When the man didn't do anything, Gage kicked the gun free of his hand. "Roll over."

"Fuck you," he said. "What the hell did you do to my tool?"

"That thing was a mess," he snapped. "Not only should there never be a license for something like that but you should never, ever use that around anyone."

"Oh, and like you're such a boy scout." He sat up.

Immediately Gage stepped back, staying out of his reach. "If you think you'll go anywhere, you're wrong."

"If you think I'm alone," he mimicked in a mocking tone, "you're wrong."

At that, Gage instinctively took a step to the side, so he could see the door that he had entered through. "That's fine. I'm totally happy to have you assholes come on in, so I can take you all out. How dare you come in after that poor woman. Haven't you done enough to her?"

"You don't have a clue what you're talking about."

"I do," he replied. "I really do. And, not only that, you have no idea who all we have."

"I don't really care if you've got that bitch and her kid," he snapped. "She was getting to be a problem anyway. I didn't really want to have to kill the kid, but, you know, what will you do?"

"That's all there was to it, *huh*? Is that the kind of guy you are? You just take orders and kill somebody completely innocent like that?"

"Hell, I don't know about innocent. I don't even know why the idiots picked her up," he muttered. "Surely there was a better deal somewhere along the line."

"Yeah, I'm sure there was." Gage shook his head. "What kind of a crew are you guys anyway?"

"Ones doing a job," he replied in a nonchalant way. "And if you think that girlfriend of yours will survive, you're wrong."

"My girlfriend?" he asked, his brows furrowed.

"The one in the bathtub back there." He nodded in that direction. "I'll just finish you off and then go take care of her finally."

"Well, she's already long gone," Gage noted, "so good luck finding her."

"I found her this time, didn't I?"

"Yeah, you did." Gage's head tilted to the side. "What did you do, put a tracker on her?"

He shrugged. "We wouldn't have had to do anything, if they'd gotten her in the first place."

"Yeah, so then you went and killed some other woman because she resembled this one? That was not a cool move."

"We really thought we had her that time. What a bunch of idiots," he said in disgust. "I almost quit this job entirely because my reputation is everything. And to think they went and screwed it up so badly and killed the wrong person because they couldn't ID the right one?" He shook his head. "It just doesn't make sense." he said, almost inviting Gage to be a part of his amusement.

"Nothing's funny about any of this," Gage replied. "That poor innocent woman is dead, and you're after another one, plus you kidnapped one with a kid, for Christ's sake. That'll traumatize the kid for life."

"And that's why I shoot them," he replied. "I mean, who wants to live with that kind of shit crawling up your ass every day and night? They are better off dead. I just put them out of their misery."

Gage struggled to keep his cool, while hearing that. "Well, you don't need to worry about them either. They're gone too."

At that, the man's eyebrows raised. "You think you'll just save everybody?"

"I'll try," he replied.

"Oh, there we go, that do-gooder attitude, even in the face of the fact that you've already lost." He laughed.

"I haven't lost anything yet," Gage argued.

"Sure you have. According to the people I work for, you've already lost three-quarters of your team. But then I guess guys like you don't really care about that. You're all in it for that macho loyalty bullshit, but that won't keep you warm at night."

"If it did, what difference does it make to you?" Gage asked. "And you should be considering that yourself."

"Why?" he asked. "They need me."

"Do you know how many of your guys I've heard say that in the last few days?" Gage replied. "What kind of loyalty are they generating from you that you actually think you're special?"

"I am special," he snapped. "They don't like killing."

"And you do?" Gage asked him.

"Hey, why not? You'll die sometime, so what difference does it make if I speed up the process?"

"Well, that's just a shitty way to look at life," Gage murmured quietly.

"Whatever, besides, if you're going to shoot me, just shoot me now," he murmured. "You know you can't do what you really want to do. Which is torturing me."

"Why can't I?" He frowned.

"Because you're far too honorable." He gave an obvious eye roll, heavy sarcasm evident in his voice. "See? You guys are all the same. I've killed a lot of you too."

"Yeah, so you want to tell me who?" he asked. Off to the side, Gage saw Tasha shifting and crawling, getting herself farther away from this guy. But she was close, paying attention.

The man shrugged. "Well, I killed the one down in DC who worked for the DOD. He was part of this special unit of yours, and they needed him taken out." He paused. "Then there was the entire team."

"Did you have anything to do with that?" Gage asked, clicking the revolver, so he could pull the trigger faster.

He laughed. "That would be way too easy for you, wouldn't it?" he replied, with a headshake. "No, unfortunately I can't claim that, as much as I'd like to. Besides, that's hardly a success, since it's not like they killed them."

"No?"

"They said something about it being just as good, but I didn't get it. Not to worry. They probably just had a different kind of torture in mind."

"I'm sure that's what they told you guys, but they're all bullshitters. They aren't strong enough to do the job." Gage added, "I'd really like to know what this is all about."

"I would too," he said. "When you find out, you want to tell me?"

Gage was getting nowhere with this smart-ass. "Were you only contracted to kill this woman?"

"Well, and take care of the kid," he added. "They were looking to keep the other woman, but I didn't think that was a good idea. Keeping prisoners is bad news for everybody. Once you get caught having them, there's really no way to prove that you didn't have anything to do with it." He shrugged. "But, hey, they didn't want to listen to a pro."

"But you're not a pro, are you? You don't have any experience."

"I've got plenty of experience," he replied in an ugly tone.

"Ah, so it matters to you that you have the experience that's needed for the job."

"Everybody needs the experience to prove that they can

do the job," he said in disgust. "Don't try to fob me off and try to make it sound like I'm doing nothing but talking out my ass. I get it, but we're hearing of other cases around the world. I've been stuck here in Manchester," he added, "but there was talk about a job in Texas. Some loose thread they would have to tie up. I was thinking I might take them up on that one"—he smirked—"but I guess it depends on what you're up to."

"You mean, whether I'll let you go or not."

"Yeah, why not?" he asked. "You got your girl, plus the others, so what difference does it make?"

"Yeah, but you'll come back and try again," Gage replied.

"I might at that," he said. "I just might."

"So, why would I let you go?" Gage asked.

"Because that's the kind of guys you are, according to them anyway. Plus all the intel we've gathered suggests that you're sort of an honorable lot. Whereas we aren't handicapped in the same way that you are."

"Why, because you don't have any morals or ethics?"

"Something like that." He shrugged again. "It's not like money is our king by any means, and there's a certain number of people I wouldn't kill, you know? My own family for one. And I know some of these guys have actually done that to their own kin, which, honestly, that's just gross."

"It is just gross," Gage agreed quietly, hoping to keep this guy talking. The more they learned, the better. "And of course then there's the war-torn countries," Gage murmured, "and all that shit that they're pulling."

"Yeah, I heard something about that, but, when I asked about it, they denied anything to do with anything but in the European countries," he noted. "I mean, that's why I had to go take care of the guy in DC."

"Ah, right, the DOD operative."

"Yeah, you know he used to go to gay bars, and notice how I used past tense in a nice way." He laughed. "That just makes people so easy to pick off and to take care of," he murmured. "They're so worried about anybody finding out that they try to do it all so secretly, which really delays identification. It's all good though. I like shit like that. You know they think that it makes them special, but really it just makes them stupid."

"He was a good man, you know," Gage said.

"I don't know if he was or not," he admitted, "and I don't really give a shit either way. He needed to go, so we took him out."

"So who makes the decision as to who needs to go?" Gage asked.

"I don't know who it is," he stated. "And I'm not too bothered about finding out. The more I know, the more I can tell under torture. So, as you know, it's much better if I don't hear anything."

"Because you like to talk, I presume."

"I do tend to go a little bit overboard sometimes," he replied, with an odd tone. "Which is another reason I don't want to know anything."

"And you think that you'll be safe now, after they know that you've been here and have been caught?"

"They don't know jack shit." He laughed.

"You said you weren't alone."

"I'm not. They're out there, waiting for me. And, when I don't come out, they'll assume I'm dead," he explained, "because I won't be taken alive, and they know it."

"Really?" Gage asked, "so you plan on killing yourself

right now or what?"

He looked around the room. "There's just you and that girl who's still half drugged, so that's hardly anything worth me even fighting about. I can take you out in a couple minutes flat."

Gage wasn't sure if that was just bravado or if this guy had some secret weapon, but Gage wouldn't get any closer and didn't want to take the chance because he was still not at peak performance, which he really needed to be in order to handle something like this. He cursed himself for not being quite there yet. Because, damn it, he really wanted to just blow off this guy's head, if not literally at least with a couple really solid punches.

He'd had the nerve to come back after poor Lorelei, who hadn't done anything to anyone. "So tell me. Why all the repeated efforts to kill Lorelei?"

"She was connected to you guys, one of those loose threads. And I'm still trying to prove to the guys that I belong on the team," he added. "So they were sending me off to do these outlying threads, just to make their life a little easier. They'd have gotten to her eventually, but I just sped up the process a bit."

"*Nice,*" Gage replied. "Of course, if you'd waited, she wouldn't have had any idea that somebody was after her."

"Yeah, but you know? It's nice when you have a bit of chase, and you get to have a little fun at the same time," he chuckled. And then, with his arms crossed, he got more serious. "Shall we get on with this?"

"What is it you want me to do?" Gage asked.

"Well, shoot me, punch me, something," he suggested. "I mean, this is boring right now. And you can't handle everything from over there."

Gage glanced at Tasha, who was sitting up a bit now, but looking pretty rough. "How are you doing?"

"I feel like shit." She used the chair to pull herself up, then sagged into the seat.

"Yeah, you don't look all that great. You think you can handle a gun on him?"

She brightened and looked at their intruder with interest. "Do I get to shoot him too?"

Gage laughed. "I don't think anybody will argue about that, except for the guys who probably want to shoot him themselves."

"Whatever. They can take their turn," she murmured. She stepped forward and, still shaky, declined his gun and pulled her own from the holster at her back.

Gage silently thanked Damon for setting her up with a concealed weapon.

"I presume you'll secure him?" she asked Gage.

"Absolutely," Gage replied.

"Nice try," said the guy, coming up off the ground, but Gage was waiting for him.

Gage stuck his jaw out, as his right fist came up in a sudden move. As the guy ducked to avoid the fist coming his way, Gage took him out with a high kick, and the fight was over before it ever really began.

With the gunman now unconscious, Gage walked over, grabbing zip straps from one of the tables of equipment that they had. He turned and quickly secured the man with several of them. Then Gage stepped back, and taking a deep breath, looked over at Tasha. "Thanks for the help," he told her. "None of us are operating at 100 percent, and, as much as I hate to admit it, I wasn't sure I could secure him without backup."

"I get it," she said. "Now, if he's secure, I need to go check on Damon."

He looked at her in surprise, and she shrugged. "Last I knew, he was watching the perimeter outside, but it is odd that he hasn't checked in."

"I haven't seen hide nor hair of him," she said.

Together, they raced back to their rooms, searching as they went. Inside, they found Damon sprawled on the floor, unconscious.

"Shit." She bent down and felt for his vitals. "He's alive, but he's definitely not conscious."

"I think this energy overload hit a lot of us," he murmured. "He just might need some recovery time." He helped Tasha get Damon onto the bed.

She looked up at Gage. "I want to stay here with him for a bit. Are you okay with that?"

"Stay," he agreed. "Keep me posted, especially if there is no change after a bit. I have to go after Lorelei, but I want to check on Sophia. You'll need to watch her too."

"Sure, I'll come and help with that," she stated, and together the two of them managed to get Sophia, who was also still unconscious, onto her bed. "Where's Wade?" she asked.

"He's out there guarding Calum's kid and Calum's wife." Tasha looked at him in shock. Gage shrugged. "I know. Surprised me too. It's the first I've heard about it. But these assholes kidnapped them and brought them here and stuck them in another room in this same damn building."

"Jesus," Tasha said. "Do you ever get the feeling they're almost making fun of us?"

"Yet we keep picking them off," he noted.

"Maybe so, but they keep getting to us."

"Not after this," he reassured her. "We're getting closer.

I promise." She didn't say anything but walked back to check on Damon and gently closed their bedroom door. Gage quickly called Terk. "Where's Wade?"

"Is he not there?"

"No," Gage replied. "Last I knew he was still with Calum's family, but I need to find him. Sophia is unconscious, but we got her to her bed, but she'll want Wade when she wakes up. And I want to get Calum's family in here safely."

"Wade should be here any moment," Terk noted. "He got hung up with traffic. There's a big accident between us."

"Wait, but he was just outside this same damn building."

"Yes, and then he took Mariana on a circular route to get them away, so nobody would know where she was. It was an attempt to stop people from following them, and then he got hung up in traffic."

"Well, he needs to get here fast," Gage snapped. "Damon must have come in at some point, and he ended up unconscious too. Tasha is awake now and is looking after both Damon and Sophia, and I need to go after Lorelei."

"You go," Terk motioned. "If everybody's in their beds recuperating right now, nothing bad can happen. And don't use just zip straps on that asshole. Make sure he's out cold and will stay that way for a while. You know where the drugs are, if you need them."

"Actually that's a great idea." Gage disconnected their call, and he headed back where his unconscious gunman lay. He checked out the drug supply in the medicine kit and found the one that he needed. He quickly administered an injection and then using rope, tied him up more securely in a hogtied position, so he shouldn't get out.

He didn't know what this guy's skill set was. But, with Terk's team not operating with any finesse these days, Gage didn't want to take any chances. And, with one last glance around, he let Tasha know where he was going and how he'd left the gunman; then Gage hightailed it out of here. What he didn't know was where the hell Lorelei had gone. He ran through the building, following her tracks. Dashing out the back door, he called out to her.

"Are you here, Lorelei? Where are you? It's safe now." But he heard nothing but an empty hollow stillness. With his stomach sinking, and hoping she had just continued to run as far and as fast as she could to get away, he contacted Terk telepathically this time. *Any sign of her?*

Nothing.

I'm not getting a good feeling about this.

Neither am I, Terk said, his tone heavy. *I'm getting other energies.*

You mean, she raced out of this damn building only to get caught again? Gage asked.

Yes, Terk said quietly. *I think so. I'll call my brother.*

What'll that do? Gage cried out in frustration.

So you can get satellite feeds. You really have no other help right now, Terk noted. *You'll have to go back inside, find her trail, and go after her.*

Gage hesitated at that.

You can do this, Terk urged.

This is what you meant, isn't it? Gage asked quietly.

Yes, I'm afraid so, damn it. Did you work on building that bond?

Sure, he confirmed, *as much as I could. It's not like I've had time to sit here and do nothing else.*

I know, he murmured. *It's all right, just do what you can.*

But it wasn't all right, and they both knew it. *I'll find her*, Gage promised Terk, and himself. Then Gage called out to the world around him. "You guys can run, but you can't hide," he shouted. "You hurt a hair on her head, and I'll make sure you don't live to see another day." It sounded like laughter filled his head, but he knew it was just that same old voice mocking him, as always. That voice of his own insecurity, the voice that said he wasn't as good as the rest on this team. That voice that said, "Hey, if you really could do this, Terk wouldn't have to tell you what to do. You'd be doing it already."

Gage had been fighting that same damn voice for a very long time and was getting damn pissed off at it.

Closing his eyes, he reached out with his heart. "Lorelei, where are you?" he murmured. He turned slowly in multiple directions, trying to find out which direction she might have gone in. He was trying to pick up the energy that she had left behind. All energy had a signature, and all energy left spores behind. He just had to lock on to the right one and to track it backward.

As he turned, slowly and carefully, all of a sudden, he felt something. He shifted back ever-so-slightly, then opened his eyes and stared at a parking lot down the block. He picked up his feet, and he ran. He didn't know where he was going; he just knew he had to go, and he had to go now. He only hoped that he got there before it was too late.

CHAPTER 10

LORELEI WOKE UP with something over her head, her hands and feet tied, and her body jolting from side to side. It took a few minutes for her brain to register the fact that she was in a moving vehicle. From the open area around her, it seemed either she was in a spacious trunk or she was in something like a van. She couldn't move her hands or her feet, but at least she didn't have something around her mouth, so she could breathe. There was complete darkness when she tried to peer through the fabric. She wasn't sure what was going on, but, damn, she felt pretty rough. She wanted to cry out but was more intent on listening.

She heard one person breathe and snuffle every once in a while, but that was it. She wasn't hearing a second person. Why would they have taken her? If the intent was to kill her, then why bother taking her like this? And the only thought that came to mind was that they wanted somebody to come after her. They would use her as bait.

With her fingers, she tried to see if her phone was still in her pocket. It felt like it probably was, but that didn't mean she could get it out when she needed to. Her hands were tied behind her. Although her wrists were secured tightly together, they were almost below her butt. Moving silently, she shifted, grateful that she had always been limber. Then she slid her arms under her butt and pulled them around, so that now her hands were in front of her.

Maybe they wouldn't recognize that she had changed the position of her hands. Now she managed to dig her phone from her pocket. Holding her phone up next to the hood on her face, she realized she could barely see through the black fabric but instead pushed the fabric up just enough that she could glance around.

With that done, she disabled the ringer on her cell, then turned on the phone and quickly turned off all notifications and sounds. She confirmed she was in the back of a van, with a whole pile of other gear and just one other person, the driver.

She quickly sent off a text, letting Gage know what had happened. Then she pulled the hood back down and stuffed her phone in her bra. She laid here, waiting, and soon the vehicle turned a quick left and then a right and came up a short but distinct rise and back down again.

Between the movements of the vehicle and the change in the sounds, she figured she might be in some car park. She waited for the engine to shut off. When it did, he got out of this vehicle and walked away. She immediately pulled the hood back up over her head, so she could watch him. He walked around outside, while he was on his phone.

She wasn't even sure what she was supposed to do, but she looked frantically for something that could be used as a weapon. She found a screwdriver, which she grabbed, and also a saw. She looked at it, frowned, and then, holding the saw with her knees and her feet, she moved the rope around her wrists back and forth over the teeth of the saw, trying to cut it. She got most of the way through when she heard him approaching again. She immediately worked harder and harder and had just cut it through when the side door opened up. She shoved the saw at him and bolted. But her feet were still tied up with rope, so she fell to the ground.

He laughed, then grabbed her by her pants, picked her up, and heaved her back into the van. "Smart," he said in an admiring voice. "Stupid too, but smart."

"Let me go," she cried out, fiercely glaring at him. He pulled the hood back down over her face, but she immediately punched out and tried to hit and kick at him.

The blow came out of nowhere and stunned her. She collapsed into the van.

"Why the hell do you think I'll let you go at this point?" he asked in a conversational tone. "Besides, now you've seen my face, so that was really not a smart move."

She froze, as she thought about it. "The other guy said that he was supposed to kill me."

"Yeah, he was, but apparently he's a worthless little piece of shit who can't do a job," he snapped. "Not to worry. He won't be bothering you anymore."

She hesitated. "Did you kill him?"

"Not yet but I will."

"I don't think he thinks that you'll kill him. In fact, he seemed to think he was the boss."

"Well, he's a long way from being the boss, so don't you worry about him," he argued. "His days are numbered. It might not be today or tomorrow"—he paused—"but rest assured. He won't survive the weekend."

She wanted to sigh with relief, but, at the same time, she worried because, if it was that easy for these guys to kill, they clearly had no remorse over any of it. "So you just kill anyone then?" she asked in a timid voice.

"Just those I get paid for," he replied.

"But it makes no sense that someone would pay to have

me killed," she wailed.

"In your case I think it was just tidying up," he muttered. "And I hired that first idiot to do the job, but he obviously failed. Now the second and third have as well."

"Yeah. You think?"

He laughed. "That's all right. It's temporary."

"I'm surprised you're as calm about it as you are," she murmured.

"No, I'm not calm about it at all," he snapped in a harsh voice. "They always get what's coming to them."

She nodded. "So then why didn't you just kill me back there?"

"Because now," he explained, "I want to capture whoever's coming after you. We thought we'd taken out everybody, but apparently a couple survived. They were in comas and not expected to live when we did the last search. We made sure a couple of them didn't survive," he muttered, "but it was our understanding that everything was taken care of. But instead these assholes just keep popping up, like bad pennies."

She smiled at that. "They're pretty good at it," she muttered.

"Yeah, they sure are," he agreed. "And that's just too damn bad because now they're starting to piss me right off. They are causing me all kinds of trouble. I took a job, and I did it, and it should have been over with."

"Well, apparently you didn't do your job that well either," she muttered.

"Don't start getting lippy with me," he said, "unless you want to get beat up some." He was clearly frustrated with the situation. "I don't particularly care either way. Nobody said you had to be untouched or not taken care of before the job was done, so an awful lot of things could happen to you that you won't like," he snapped. "So just keep being a smart-ass, and see how far it gets you."

She immediately shut up then because there was no doubting his meaning on that one.

He laughed. "Smart cookie, *huh*. Maybe I'll have some fun with you after all. There's got to be some damn good thing to come out of all this bullshit."

Her heart froze, as she thought about it. "Please don't," she whispered.

"Don't worry about it," he said. "It depends on if I have time or not anyway."

She could hardly sit here and wish that he wouldn't have time, but she also wanted to make sure that he would never get hold of her. She whispered, "Who are you waiting for anyway?"

"The team that was supposed to be annihilated and wasn't," he replied. "Don't be stupid."

At that, she didn't say anything for a few moments. "Can I go to the bathroom?"

"Yeah, have a squat," he said, "like I give a shit."

She gasped.

He laughed. "God, you women are such timid idiots," he murmured. "Don't worry. It won't be long. I don't know what these guys have for special skills, but my boss is definitely worried about them following us. So, if we can take any out right now, I will." And, with that, he pulled out weapons from the boxes and bags that he had in the back beside her.

She had gotten a look round before, and, even now, with a hood on, she heard him arming up. "Wow, you came loaded for bear." Her voice trembled.

"Yeah, … I wasn't going to, but they seem to think these guys are some hard-ass numbers. So I won't go up against a bear with a knife," he noted, with a caustic tone.

"And me?"

"Oh, you just get to sit here," he said. "But, if you run, I'll shoot you. You can't do very much running when your feet are tied like that, but, if you'll be good, I won't tie your hands behind you."

"Please don't," she murmured.

He laughed. "And you really think I'll just let you sit here on your own? Jesus, what an idiot," He tied her hands again, with zip straps this time. "Yeah, they hurt like the dickens and start to cut your skin," he stated, "but, hey, I understand you need to try. So you do you." With that, he left the door open and sauntered off to the side.

"Where will you go?" she called out.

"Hide someplace where I have a full view," he replied. "Remember. If you do anything wrong, I'll just pick you off. I don't care either way. The fact of the matter is, if you're dead, it's easier for me. One less thing, you know? They'll still come after you anyway. Plus they'll make more mistakes if you are dead. Emotions and all that." He chuckled, as he disappeared.

She listened hard, tracking the direction he traveled, trying to figure out what to do. After going to the bathroom, she settled back inside the van with the metal of the vehicle between her and whatever direction he'd gone. She pushed up the hood again, pulled out her phone, glad she had stashed it in her bra. Maybe it made no difference, or maybe her kidnapper was tracking it, she didn't know. But she immediately sent out a message to Gage and to Terk. **It's a trap.**

She gave a quick explanation and shut off her phone. She had no idea where she was, except that she was in some ground-floor car park. Other than that, she saw nothing to identify her location or to give her any clues.

She took her phone out and took several photos and sent them to give the guys some idea. But, other than that, she didn't know what else to do. She sent a message to Tasha, telling her as well. Then Lorelei sat here and waited. She knew they would come; no way they wouldn't. It was just a matter of who would come and who would survive this battle of wits.

She knew who she was hoping for, but this asshole was a little too comfortable with this whole scenario. Nauseatingly so. She knew the guys were too, but she didn't know how well.

They'd been operatives for a long time, but everybody made mistakes, and the fact that the bad guys had her would make Gage a whole lot more sensitive to the outcome. She looked down at her phone, then sent him a text. **I love you. Maybe don't come.**

She almost heard him snorting in her head at that. She smiled. **Never mind. I don't want to be a martyr. I just want to be safe, but I don't want you hurt in the meantime.**

Having a connection like that with him was just so damn special. But she also knew that she couldn't count on it. She shifted to look out into the world around her. No sign of the gunman. And nothing she could do. If she got up and left, she knew for sure she'd be taken down. Then she thought about it and looked around to see just how much there was to hide behind. Maybe nothing, but maybe she could get out of here, and maybe she would be fine.

She looked for the saw again, hoping it landed in the van with her. Finding it, she worked on her ties on her hands and her feet this time. It took a while, and she was sweating, worried about the noise she might be making. But, with a big sigh, her hands and feet were free.

She shuffled around in the van, shifting to her knees to get a better look. There was a little bit of cover off to the side, if she could just sneak through the passenger side. *Maybe it'd work.* As she decided to head toward the front of the van, a shot came through and completely destroyed the windshield. Swearing, she settled back again.

"So much for that idea," she grumbled.

Lorelei actually thought that maybe she could just hop in and drive away. Okay, so he wasn't stupid, and he wouldn't just let her walk away either. Swearing again, she settled back down, now wondering if she could sneak through the passenger door by crouching forward. By that time, she was pretty damn sure that the guys should have been here already.

At least one of them anyway. If they came.

She hated the thought deep in her heart of hearts that maybe nobody was coming.

GAGE COULD SEE Lorelei up ahead. She was restless, looking at options, and he didn't want her to do anything stupid. He'd heard the windshield explode, and obviously she had considered getting into the front seat, either to exit the vehicle on the far side or to just drive away. Everybody would have considered it. But guys like this, they set up things like that so they could deliberately shoot somebody just for the fun of it.

The element of a bit of a hunt was going on here, and Gage would take down this asshole who was after her. Gage had no idea who had hired him, and that'd be yet another piece of this damn puzzle, but first Gage had to save her. These guys had targeted her again and again for no reason, other than perhaps her association with him and his team, and that had been nothing but hell since. That was something he couldn't live with.

He shifted his angle, until he caught the gunman again in his sights. He was protected enough that Gage couldn't get a clear shot, but, if the gunman raised his rifle toward her one more time, Gage would take him out regardless.

As it was, Gage shifted his position slightly, and almost instantly the gunman turned toward him.

His voice called out, "I can see you're here. You won't get her out alive this way." He laughed, taunting Gage.

Gage didn't answer. He studied the gunman's position, and it was good in that he was on the high side, so it was harder for Gage to shoot upward. The gunman was also slightly behind a huge pillar, so that was even better for him. But Gage himself was no fool. He also had a little bit going for him.

He closed his eyes and sent out a probe toward Lorelei. When she jolted at his touch, he smiled, realizing some of his strength was coming back. He didn't know if it was coming from Terk in this case or not. But Gage turned the same probe over to Lorelei's kidnapper, had his probe come up around behind him and poked him gently.

The gunman bolted to his feet, looking around. "What the hell was that?" he asked. "Where are you?" He started shooting in all directions, including the van, but Gage was no longer at the same spot. He watched from his new position, a good twenty feet closer. The guy was spooked now, and that's just how Gage wanted him. He poked him with a probe again, listening as he freaked out.

"What the hell is this?" the gunman asked. "I don't know what boogeyman bullshit this is," he shouted. "Get your ass out here, and fight like a normal person."

But no way in hell Gage would do that. He waited and waited and then, just when it looked like the gunman was calming down, Gage did it again. This time he grabbed the cord coming off the kidnapper's spine and gave it a rattle. The guy came running out of his hiding spot, freaking out and screaming. Almost instantly a shot rang out and hit him square in the forehead.

Swearing, Gage turned to look where the shot came from—another vehicle on the street. Gage took off running toward the getaway car, knowing there was no way he'd catch it, but he raced forward, trying. Then a series of shots came, several of which hit the kidnapper's van, and Gage knew that was bad news. He immediately turned as the vehicle took off, heading for freedom. And Gage raced toward Lorelei. He came around the van, only to see her lying there, with blood pouring from the corner of her mouth. She looked up at him and coughed, more blood coming out.

"Jesus," he said, "hold on. Just hold on."

She looked at him, tears slowly running from her eyes. "I had hope," she whispered.

"Don't try to talk," he told her. "You just let me work on this. We've got this." She gave him a half smile and slowly closed her eyes. He could see the wound in the chest in his mind, and he was already screaming out for help from anybody who was there on the ethers, anybody who could help him.

Terk answered, *Remember exactly what happened.*

I remember. I remember.

I'm here, Terk said. *Now breathe with me.*

Breathing and focusing on Terk's energy settled Gage down a bit.

Now, Terk stated calmly, *seal up that wound.*

How the hell do I do that? he asked, but he could already feel energy surging through him.

Remember. We're all one, Terk added. *That's the first law of killing, isn't it? You can join them and take them down very easily. You were just playing with that.*

"Look what good that did me," he yelled. "She's dying."

Not yet, Terk replied, quiet and calm.

Too calmly. Gage wanted to rage at him; Gage wanted to scream. *I shouldn't have done it. I should have just taken him out.*

You were trying to save her. You were trying to keep this guy alive so we could get answers. I get it, Terk replied. *Sometimes even our best intentions backfire. And we weren't expecting yet another person.*

What if she dies?

Do you see her energy?

He could; it was right in front of him, even though his eyes were closed. He placed his hands over her heart.

That's good, Terk stated. *Now slow down that bleeding.*

It was a moment before Gage realized somebody was beside him, actively working on her physically. He opened his eyes to see Merk.

"Field medic," Merk explained. "Been doing it way-the-hell too long."

"Can you help her?"

"Yep, I can, but you keep doing whatever the hell you're doing." He shook his head. "And, no, I don't want to know what it is. My brother is fucking amazing, and the fact that more people like him are out there is just mind-boggling."

"You mean. you aren't one of us?" Gage asked, with half a laugh.

Merk shot him a look. "Bite your tongue."

And, with that, Gage closed his eyes and focused. It was hard; it was damn hard, but he was doing everything he could to try to save her. "It's not that easy."

"Nope," Merk said. "I get it."

Gage watched, as she was administered some pretty rough field medicine. She stared up at him, but no recognition was in her eyes.

"Keep talking to her. Keep doing whatever you're doing," Merk repeated. "It looks like it's gone in through the side of her lung." He slapped something atop the surface of the wound, and she immediately started breathing easier. "But there was another nick on her neck." Merk turned his attention to that.

"Jesus," Gage groaned.

"Stop. Stay focused. We've got this. You do your thing. I'll do mine." Merk spared him a stern glance.

Gage took several slow deep breaths. "I'm glad you're here."

"Me too," Merk muttered, "and that's because of my brother. He said some of my skills would be needed. Wouldn't it be nice if we actually knew ahead of time, so we could have things like an ambulance nearby?" he said bitterly.

"It's not that easy. It's not that simple, and we never

know that much detail," Gage murmured.

"You just stay connected and keep her alive. She doesn't know how much she needs you yet, but you'll be put through the mill over this," Merk stated.

"In what way?"

But Terk answered his question. *She'll have to go through surgery, and you'll have to go through it with her.*

You know they won't even let me in the room, Gage replied in his mind to Terk.

They won't know you're there, Terk replied.

Almost immediately an ambulance raced to them. She was soon transferred onto a gurney and headed down the street. Gage stood here, blood all over his hands. Merk was at his side but immediately led Gage toward his vehicle.

"My brother says to just keep you moving in her direction and to keep you as close as possible," he explained. "You keep doing whatever it is you're doing."

"You have no idea what I'm doing," he wailed, his voice slow like molasses.

"I get it," Merk nodded. "Every time I'm with my brother, I learn something new. I'm taking you to the hospital, so you just focus on staying connected with her."

It was like being connected by an elastic band. The vehicle ahead went around the corner, and he went around it as well, just behind it, because Merk was driving like a crazy man, trying to keep up.

And Gage couldn't argue because all he wanted to do was tell Merk to go faster and faster. She was in the ambulance ahead, still alive, but her life force was slowly welling up and out of her. He fought with everything he could. He lost track of time, lost track of hours, lost track of whatever the hell was going on. He saw the lights, heard the sirens, saw the blood, and the doctors in white lab coats. He was aware of the trolleys rolling down the hallways, the panic, the racing, the controlled chaos, and then suddenly the lights from a surgical room.

And he was still here, still connected. Terk urged Gage to stay on, to stay strong, and to hold on to her life force, to tell her how much he loved her and to not let go because letting go would be fatal. And that was something Gage just couldn't handle. He hung on with all his heart, whispering in her mind all the while.

Fight for me, baby. Do your damnedest to stay here. And then he heard this weird snapping *pop*, and he saw everything fading in front of him. And before he realized it, there was just darkness. Frantic, he called out for her. *No, no, don't! Get back here!* he roared in her mind.

And then came the faintest of voices.

I'm here, she said. *Let go.* And, with that, he collapsed and crashed onto the floor beside her bed.

CHAPTER 11

LORELEI OPENED HER eyes and stared up at the ceiling above her, but then the sight disappeared. She gurgled an odd sound, a funny sound. A voice immediately hopped into her head.

Stay calm, someone said.

Who is this? she murmured, yet it didn't happen out loud.

Terk.

She closed her eyes. *Is Gage okay?*

Well, he might be, just as long as you are, he added, with a note of humor.

Where is he?

Beside you.

She opened her eyes and shifted, catching just the barest hint of a man lying beside her. *Good God, is he okay?* She started to fight for consciousness.

Stop.

Instantly she froze.

He's okay. He's drained. You're okay. You're drained. Just close your eyes, and go back to sleep.

She wanted to fight him, wanted to argue with him. And then there was no argument at all, and she was just out cold. When she surfaced the next time, the same thing happened, as all the fight left her, and she was back under within minutes. She didn't know whether Terk was doing something to push her under or if something else was going on. But she didn't have the will or any physical energy to even fight it off.

When she surfaced for the third time, her awareness happened faster. She looked to see that Gage still slept at her side. She reached out a hand. "Are you okay?" she whispered to him.

An odd murmur came from beside her. Then he opened his eyes, looked at her, blinked several times, and slowly sat up. He stared around the room, confused, only to have his gaze zoom back to her. "Are you okay?" he whispered gently.

"Well, I might be," she murmured. "I'm not sure. Everything feels off. It's odd." And there was that voice in her head again.

That's because you're running on double energy right now. You may feel a weird light-headedness, a euphoria almost. You need to stay quiet and to let your body heal.

She looked down at Gage. "There's this voice in my head. I think it's Terk, telling me to stay in bed and to heal."

Gage smiled. "Yeah, that'll be Terk, and he's telling me the same thing."

"If you don't mind, I'll just go out again." And she collapsed back down.

GAGE SHIFTED, UNTIL he was upright. He looked over at Lorelei, and she looked much better, but he had no idea what the hell had happened. But since he was not feeling all that great himself, it was all he could do to get his own head reattached. "Terk, where are you?"

Just then the door opened, and Merk stepped in. He took one look at Gage, and a big grin flashed across his face. "There you are. I almost lost you."

"Me?" Gage asked. "We almost lost her."

"Yeah, you almost lost her too," he noted, but then smiled with satisfaction. "But we saved you both, so it's all good, and you'll live to fight another day."

"God, I get so tired of fighting sometimes," he muttered.

"But sometimes we don't get a choice," Merk added, "because our loved ones are being targeted."

At that, Gage's gaze immediately flipped back to Lorelei. "Did we catch the guy who did this?"

"The guy who took her is dead. Remember?" Merk tilted his head. "The cops are all over that."

"*Great*," Gage muttered. "They'll really be wondering what the hell's going on."

"No, not yet," Merk replied. "They think it's just a kidnapping gone wrong."

"Nice, I mean, the parting of thieves or some such thing. The cops should buy that, you know?"

"Exactly," Merk agreed. "We know better of course."

Gage looked at him. "Has anybody tracked down that vehicle?"

"Didn't need to. It was abandoned not even a block away."

"Of course, a getaway vehicle to another vehicle. Are they running out of bad guys yet?" he asked in disgust.

"Nope, not yet. But we did get a new line to tug on this kidnapper. Your hackers are working on that," he explained. "And we still have the one captive back at the compound."

At that, Gage lit up. "That's right. I left him alive, didn't I?"

"Yeah, that's pretty decent of you." Merk smiled. "Apparently you have a habit of not bringing anybody home."

Gage winced. "It might have happened a time or two."

"Right. Well, in this case," Merk added, "it's a good thing you held off. Now we can interrogate him and hopefully find out something more."

"I hope so." Gage looked over at Lorelei. "She needs to be under guard."

"Well, guess where you're staying?"

Gage winced and nodded. "I guess that's fair. Besides, we don't know that somebody else will make another attempt."

"I would expect that they will," Merk agreed quietly. "Not only can they not leave her alive but they can't leave their reputations tarnished like that."

"Yeah. Whoever is hiring them is making a laughingstock of them all."

"And that's bad for business."

"I don't really give a shit about their reputations," Gage snapped in a vicious tone. "I'm so pissed off and fed up with all this shit that I just want these attempts on Lorelei's life to stop."

"Got it. So you're on guard duty," Merk stated. "Feel free to rest as you need to, but, at the same time, expect us to contact you soon. We'll go have a talk with the friend you left us."

"*Great*," Gage moaned. "And I get to miss all the fun."

"You do, indeed." Merk laughed. "On the other hand, maybe if you're lucky, you'll get another chance to take out someone here in the hospital."

"Wouldn't that be great?"

"Remember. We still need people to talk to."

Gage rolled his eyes at that. "Only if they don't do any thing stupid. If they do, I got them." And, with that, Merk left. Gage laid back down and stared up at the hospital ceiling, his fingers gently lacing with hers. "You just rest now," he murmured to the quiet room. "I'm standing watch. Don't worry. I'm here, and I will be here all the time." Maybe it was his imagination, but it seemed to him that she squeezed his fingers, even in sleep. He smiled and let his eyes drift closed again.

When he woke up the next time, an odd stillness filled the air around him. He froze, then opened his eyes to see a man standing in front of him, a gun pointed inches from his face. He swore and didn't even blink as he lifted up off the bed, grabbing the gunman's arm and turning it into the guy's chest, as the man pulled the trigger. The man fell to the ground, staring up at him, sightless. Commotion from outside the hospital room raced toward him.

Merk stepped in first, then took one look and groaned. "Jesus Christ."

"Yeah, that's how I feel. I fell asleep, then woke up to this guy with his gun in my face. I didn't like that," he snapped in a surly tone.

"Got it," Merk murmured. "You do know that you really do need to leave some of these guys alive for the rest of us."

"Hey, I left you one," he growled.

"Yeah, you did," he agreed. "And we had a little talk with him. We've turned him over to the authorities."

At that, Gage was surprised. "Really? The cops are involved now?"

"Too many dead bodies for them not to be." Merk shrugged. "At some point we have to get along with the locals. We can't just argue with them."

Gage groaned. "Are you sure? It's so much easier without their interference."

The faintest voice came from the bed. "Gage?"

He immediately placed a hand on her forehead and whispered, "I'm here. I'm here."

She opened her eyes and smiled up at him. "That's one of the best words in the dictionary," she murmured. "My favorite."

He chuckled and asked, "How are you feeling?"

"Pretty shitty," she replied, "but did I just hear a fight?"

"*Nah*," he said. "That wasn't bad enough to call a fight at all."

She shuffled upward to look around a bit and saw Merk, then the body on the floor. "Oh my God. Here too?"

"Yes, but this one's gone, and we've already taken another to the police," Merk explained, with a bright smile. "So your only job, now that we've caught the guys hunting you, is to heal."

She collapsed back onto the bed. "Well, thank God for that. Honestly, I feel like shit."

"Of course you do," Gage replied. "I'm staying here, and we're keeping an eye out, so don't you worry. You just rest."

She looked up at him. "And you'll be here?"

"I'll be right here. I promise." He leaned over and whispered against her ear, "And I don't just mean for today. I'll be here forever."

The smile on her lips was soft and tender. "You be here when you can, and the rest of the time is fine. I'll survive then too."

He loved that about her. She was always so forgiving and accepting. It was hard to argue with that, and he had no intention of it. "I mean it."

"I know you do," she said. "But I have to admit, I still feel cruddy."

"Well, the nurse is coming," Gage replied, as he saw the nurse approach. "So I'll leave you for a minute and step out in the hallway, while they check you over."

"Good. As long as you come back, that is."

"Always," he whispered, then dropped a kiss on her forehead and stepped away. He watched from the doorway as she was administered more medicine, her bandages checked, and all her vitals taken.

The nurse smiled at him and said, "You're doing a good job. Just keep it up."

He smiled, then nodded. "I'll be right here."

"Good." The nurse smiled. "I have no doubt in my mind that's why she's still alive. Because, honest to God, there's no way she should be. No way she should have survived that."

"Well, that just wasn't in the cards," he replied quietly.

She nodded, her gaze searching. "I know that, and I've seen all kinds of miracles in my life, but this is one of the biggest. You're a lucky man." Then she stopped and looked down at her patient, whose eyes were already closed. "Actually she's a very lucky woman." With that, the nurse left to tend to her next patient.

Gage walked over to the doorway, where Merk stood, and asked, "How's Calum?"

"Well, according to Terk, he's doing much better now."

"Meaning that he is up and about and is reunited with his family?"

"Yeah, I guess you guys didn't know about it, *huh*?"

"No, I didn't know about any of it." Gage gave a shake

of his head. "The secrets this team has are unbelievable."

"Maybe it had to be that way," Merk suggested. "Maybe you guys know so much or are such open books with each other that this was the only way you had to keep some little part of yourself private."

Gage nodded. "Maybe so, but I'm actually really happy that all of this is out in the open and to know that at least some of us have partners now." He looked down at Lorelei. "She's always been very special to me. And again it was one of those things that we thought we would have, after we started our new life," he murmured.

"And there is no reason not to," Merk said, "especially now."

"Well, maybe, but first we have to get through this."

"You're there. Not to worry. You're there already. You got the girl." Merk took one last look at Lorelei lying on the bed, then turned to go.

"Absolutely," Gage replied.

Just then Merk's phone rang. He pulled it out and answered, taking a few steps away. Gage waited at the bed to hear what the news update was. When Merk came back, Gage knew it wasn't good. His heart sinking, he said, "Don't tell me. The prisoner was shot to death in transport."

Merk nodded, his face grim. "A drone."

"Well, we found all kinds of drones earlier in this mess," Gage nodded, "so I guess I'm not surprised. Now what?" he asked.

"Well, we did get some information from him, and everybody is working on that." Merk squeezed Gage's shoulder. "You just focus on getting your strength back and looking after her."

"I can do that." Gage nodded. "Nowhere else I'd want to

be." And, with that, he headed back to sit down beside Lorelei, his fingers lacing with hers, and that's exactly where he'd stay, until this nightmare of a case was over. He had no intention of walking away from her ever again.

EPILOGUE

C ALUM LANCASHIRE WALKED unsteadily forward, as he entered the temporary headquarters for Terk's team here in Manchester, England. Terk was here, giving freely of his energy, and, with every step that Calum took, he was getting stronger. He was using a cane, something that he'd never used in his life, and it was hard—damn hard, in fact. It was awkward and debilitating, but, hey, he was finally upright. Nothing worse than not being on his feet. He smiled at Terk. "Thank you."

"For what?" Terk asked.

"For keeping me alive, for one. For keeping Mariana alive, for two. And for saving my kid."

"For that, you're very welcome," Terk replied. "We have a lot to catch up on. You're way behind on the news."

"Where are they?"

"They're down the hall here just a bit," he stated. "Can you make it?"

"Of course I'll make it." When they opened the door, Cal heard a gasp, and he stepped inside. There was Mariana, standing beside a double bed that contained his son, four-year-old Little Calum. Cal opened his arms, and Mariana raced forward.

"I'll leave you three alone. Cal, we'll meet up later," Terk said, turning to leave.

After he left the room, but still in the hallway as he could be heard talking to someone, Mariana whispered to her husband, "I didn't know. I'm sorry. I just didn't know."

"I got it," he murmured. "I tried to tell you."

"And now I get it." She shook her head. "It was terrible, absolutely terrible, but we're safe, and now I have you back." She squeezed him hard.

He held her close, his face buried in her beautiful soft blond hair. She always smelled like the scent of roses, and yet she swore she never used any perfume. Maybe it was a whiff of her shampoo? He didn't know, but it was stunning, and it brought back so many memories that the tears choked the back of his throat. "I'm so glad you're safe," he whispered, "and I'm so damn sorry that you and our son got caught up in this nightmare."

She shook her head. "It's fine," she said quietly. "I get it. I mean, I really do understand now."

He shook his head. "You shouldn't have to *get it*." He groaned. "At least they didn't hurt you two, thank God."

"No, but Little Calum is quite traumatized," she noted, "and I've had a hard time getting him to sleep."

"We'll find a safe place for you two, until this is over."

She pulled back ever-so-slightly, then looked up at him. "The kidnappers did mention a name. Rulrul," she murmured. "I don't know who that is but—"

At that, Terk stepped forward. "What, do you mean, *Rulrul*? What did they say?"

"Something like, 'Rulrul won't like this. He doesn't like involving kids or women.' But apparently it was a necessary tactic that they felt they had to employ."

"Now that's interesting," Terk replied. "Did you hear a last name or anything about a location?"

"Something to do with overseas, I think. I thought he meant Asia, but I don't really know."

"Did they say anything about the government? Or anything about being paid?"

"I overheard all kinds of bits and pieces," she noted. "It's obvious that they didn't worry about whether I heard or not," she murmured, "but it was pretty rough to make out words."

"Take your time. If you remember something later, no matter how insignificant, let us know," Terk replied. "I'm glad you remembered the name Rulrul."

"I only wish I had more, but I'm not sure that does any good."

"It does. Believe me. All intel does." Terk gave her a bright smile.

She held herself close against Cal.

He just wanted to hold her and to squeeze her tight. He dropped a kiss on her forehead. "I promise we'll get to the bottom of this," he told her, "and nobody will hurt Little Calum anymore. I'm so sorry."

She looked up at him, smiled, and murmured, "I know, and you aren't to blame. And maybe it's better in a way because now I understand why you walked away. I knew that you were concerned about danger to us, but I underestimated what that really meant and never expected to have it so forcibly shown to me."

"And it shouldn't have been," he snapped in a rough voice. Then he looked over at Terk.

She shook her head. "It's not Terk's fault."

"No, it's not," Calum said, "but you can bet we're all after answers. Real and final answers."

She stopped a moment, then smiled. "*Sean.*"

Both men looked at her, with quizzical expressions.

"Sean," she repeated. "One of the men they were talking with was Sean."

"Any idea in what capacity?" Terk asked.

"No, but I think he was the one who said something about Calum won't be happy."

"So, Rulrul won't be happy, and Calum won't be happy."

"I think Sean is the one who arranged for us to get picked up," she murmured. "I could be wrong though. ... I don't really know. It was mentioned just in passing, as they were leaving, and one of the guys was speaking to the other one. The one guy said, 'Sean, this is your deal.' So I presumed the other guy was Sean. He laughed and said, 'Yeah, old Calum won't be happy with me.' Oh wait." She stopped, then looked at the two men. "Then Sean said something about it being a damn fine time for it. Something like, 'I've been waiting forever.' Does any of that make sense?"

At that, Calum stiffened and pulled her tightly into his arms again, holding her close. He looked at Terk over the top of her head. "That can't be Sean Calvert, can it?"

"I suggest we find out," Terk stated quietly. "Sean has been after you for a long time."

She pulled back, looked up at her husband.

He faced her and explained, "His life is a mess, and he's always blamed me for it. It could explain him grabbing you and our son."

"Did you do something to him?" she asked.

He immediately shook his head. "No, but a guy like that is just looking for excuses. He's glommed onto me as his enemy, and that's all he cared about. We were on friendly terms at one time."

She winced. "I'm sorry. That sounds pretty rough. For you and him."

"It was very rough for him apparently," Calum noted. "I've received threats from him over the years, and I've told him several times that I had nothing to do with his problems."

"But, like you said, he doesn't want to listen."

"Right, he doesn't want to listen at all," he added. "And obviously he has let that hate boil over to something completely out of hand, and he's not prepared to even consider the truth anymore."

"No." She shook her head. "Yet he sounded normal, looked normal, if *normal* is a term applied here."

He gave her a description of a man about five-eleven, with curly blond hair and a suntan, like a surfer.

She nodded slowly. "Yeah, exactly."

"Good," he confirmed, "at least now I know who it is. This time we'll have a meet-up that only one of us will walk away from."

"Then it damn well better be you," she cried out.

"I didn't come this far to lose you and Little Calum now." He smiled. "I worked really hard to survive that blast, and I have no intention of you losing me either, but I do intend to stop somebody who has such a hate-on for me that he'll continue to be a threat to us." He paused. "This is well past the point of normal behavior, and I had nothing to do with everything that's gone wrong in his life," he murmured. "It's well past time for him to understand it." And, with that, he leaned over, kissed her gently. "Besides, I have to keep you guys safe. And I'll do whatever it takes."

She threw her arms around him. "I know you will. You're not to blame for any of this, but please don't do anything stupid."

"I won't do anything stupid." Yet he felt his own temper still simmering. "But you can sure as hell bet that I won't let myself off as easily as you let me off."

She winced. "I knew you would take it the wrong way, if I told you anything."

"It doesn't matter," he replied. "We're at the point in time now where there's literally no going back. We have to get to the bottom of everything and stop this, Sean included. We've had a ton of our people attacked, and some didn't survive," he added quietly. "We all have families, and we all want to make sure everything's good."

"I get it," she agreed. "So go off and do your thing."

He smiled. "I wanted to just stay here and be with you for a little bit." But he caught sight of Terk, who shook his head.

"As much as that would be nice," Terk said, "it's not to be. We'll bring you up to date, and we need to hunt down Sean, before he causes any more trouble." And, with that, Terk left, clearly expecting Calum to follow.

The thing was, he would. Terk had been there for Calum every step of the way, and Cal would be there for Terk now. All Calum had to do was make sure that his team hunted down Sean and took out these assholes. And then go back after the other members of his team who were still comatose. Calum would do what he could to help pull them back out, just as Terk had pulled Cal out.

It was a terrible half-living state to be in, particularly for those with their kinds of abilities, used to pushing their bodies and their minds to the fullest extent, all in the protection of others. He kissed his wife gently once more. "I'll be back in a little bit."

She smiled, then nodded. "Go on. I know you have to, and it's fine. Just make sure you come home at the end of the day." And, with that, she stepped back and gave him a tentative wave. He walked over and kissed the sleeping child on the forehead, whispering in his ear. Then Cal headed out to follow Terk.

This concludes Book 3 of Terkel's Team: Gage's Goal.

Read about Calum's Contact: Terkel's Team, Book 4

Terkel's Team: Calum's Contact (Book #4)

Welcome to a brand-new series from *USA Today* best-selling author Dale Mayer, where dark-ops SEALs have special senses and skills, needed to solve intrigue, betrayal, and … murder. A series with all the elements you've come to love, plus so much more, … including psychics!

As his career path led him into more and more danger, Calum made a decision to keep his family safe, even if it meant he would be alone in the world. But when his wife and son are kidnapped and dumped almost into his very own secret headquarters, Calum knows his safeguards haven't been enough.

Mariana didn't like Calum's decision from years ago but finally understood after her and her son are rescued from kidnappers, and she saw the dangerous level of his work. However, having him once again in her life, their family whole again, she's not willing to let him go. Not this time. If the danger would continue, … surely they were safer at his side.

Calum's abilities at an all-time low, his friends and fellow teammates injured and struggling, Calum knows he must be there for the team. Yet protecting his family comes first. But, if they don't get to the bottom of the chaos that's his current life, … no one is safe.

Find Book 4 here!
To find out more visit Dale Mayer's website.
http://smarturl.it/DMSTTCalum

Magnus: Shadow Recon (Book #1)

Deep in the permafrost of the Arctic, a joint task force, comprised of over one dozen countries, comes together to level up their winter skills. A mix of personalities, nationalities, and egos bring out the best—and the worst—as these globally elite men and women work and play together. They rub elbows with hardy locals and a group of scientists gathered close by …

One fatality is almost expected with this training. A second is tough but not a surprise. However, when a third goes missing? It's hard to not be suspicious. When the missing man is connected to one of the elite Maverick team members and is a special friend of Lieutenant Commander Mason Callister? All hell breaks loose ...

LIEUTENANT COMMANDER MASON Callister walked into the private office and stood in front of retired Navy Commander Doran Magellan.

"Mason, good to see you."

Yet the dry tone of voice, and the scowl pinching the silver-haired man, all belied his words. Mason had known Doran for over a decade, and their friendship had only grown over time.

Mason waited, as he watched the other man try to work the new tech phone system on his desk. With his hand circling the air above the black box, he appeared to hit buttons randomly.

Mason held back his amusement but to no avail.

"Why can't a phone be a phone anymore?" the commander snapped, as his glare shifted from Mason to the box and back.

Asking the commander if he needed help wouldn't make the older man feel any better, but sitting here and watching as he indiscriminately punched buttons was a struggle. "Is Helen away?" Mason asked.

"Yes, damn it. She's at lunch, and I need her to be at lunch." The commander's piercing gaze pinned Mason in place. "No one is to know you're here."

Solemn, Mason nodded. "Understood."

"Doran? Is that you?" A crotchety voice slammed into the room through the phone's speakers. "Get away from that damn phone. You keep clicking buttons in my ear. Get

Helen in there to do this."

"No, she can't be here for this."

Silence came first, then a huge groan. "Damn it. Then you should have connected me last, so I don't have to sit here and listen to you fumbling around."

"Go pour yourself a damn drink then," Doran barked. "I'm working on the others."

A snort was his only response.

Mason bit the inside of his lip, as he really tried to hold back his grin. The retired commander had been hell on wheels while on active duty, and, even now, the retired part of his life seemed to be more of a euphemism than anything.

"Damn things …"

Mason looked around the dark mahogany office and the walls filled with photos, awards, medals. A life of purpose, accomplishment. And all of that had only piqued his interest during the initial call he'd received, telling him to be here at this time.

"Ah, got it."

Mason's eyebrows barely twitched, as the commander gave him a feral grin. "I'd rather lead a warship into battle than deal with some of today's technology."

As he was one of only a few commanders who'd been in a position to do such a thing, it said much about his capabilities.

And much about current technology.

The commander leaned back in his massive chair and motioned to the cart beside Mason. "Pour three cups."

Interesting. Mason walked a couple steps across the rich tapestry-style carpet and lifted the silver service to pour coffee into three very down-to-earth-looking mugs.

"Black for me."

Mason picked up two cups and walked one over to Doran.

"Thanks." He leaned forward and snapped into the phone, "Everyone here?"

Multiple voices responded.

Curiouser and curiouser. Mason recognized several of the voices. Other relics of an era gone by. Although not a one would like to hear that, and, in good faith, it wasn't fair. Mason had thought each of these men were retired, had relinquished power. Yet, as he studied Doran in front of him, Mason had to wonder if any of them actually had passed the baton or if they'd only slid into the shadows. Was this planned with the government's authority? Or were these retirees a shadow group to the government?

The tangible sense of power and control oozed from Doran's words, tone, stature—his very pores. This man might be heading into his sunset years—based on a simple calculation of chronological years spent on the planet—but he was a long way from being out of the action.

"Mason …" Doran began.

"Sir?"

"We've got a problem."

Mason narrowed his gaze and waited.

Doran's glare was hard, steely hard, with an icy glint. "Do you know the Mavericks?"

Mason's eyebrows shot up. The black ops division was one of those well-kept secrets, so, therefore, everyone knew about it. He gave a decisive nod. "I do."

"And you're involved in the logistics behind the ICE training program in the Arctic, are you not?"

"I am." Now where was the commander going with this?

"Do you know another SEAL by the name of Mountain

Rode? He's been working for the black ops Mavericks." At his own words, the commander shook his head. "What the hell was his mother thinking when she gave him that moniker?"

"She wasn't thinking anything," said the man with a hard voice from behind Mason.

He stiffened slightly, then relaxed as he recognized that voice too.

"She died giving birth to me. And my full legal name is Mountain Bear Rode. It was my father's doing."

The commander glared at the new arrival. "Did I say you could come in?"

"Yes." Mountain's voice was firm, yet a definitive note of affection filled his tone.

That emotion told Mason so much.

The commander harrumphed, then cleared his throat. "Mason, we're picking up a significant amount of chatter over that ICE training. Most of it good. Some of it the usual caterwauling we've come to expect every time we participate in a joint training mission. This one is set to run for six months, then to reassess."

Mason already knew this. But he waited for the commander to get around to why Mason was here, and, more important, what any of this had to do with the mountain of a man who now towered beside him.

The commander shifted his gaze to Mountain, but he remained silent.

Mason noted Mountain was not only physically big but damn imposing and severely pissed, seemingly barely holding back the forces within. His body language seemed to yell, *And the world will fix this, or I'll find the reason why.*

For a moment Mason felt sorry for the world.

Finally a voice spoke through the phone. "Mason, this is Alpha here. I run the Mavericks. We've got a problem with that ICE training center. Mountain, tell him."

Mason shifted to include Mountain in his field of vision. Mason wished the other men on the conference call were in the room too. It was one thing to deal with men you knew and could take the measure of; it was another when they were silent shadows in the background.

"My brother is one of the men who reported for the Artic training three weeks ago."

"Tergan Rode?" Mason confirmed. "I'm the one who arranged for him to go up there. He's a great kid."

A glimmer of a smile cracked Mountain's stony features. He nodded. "Indeed. A bright light in my often dark world. He's a dozen years younger than me, just passed his BUD/s training this spring, and raring to go. Until his raring to go then got up and went."

Oh, shit. Mason's gaze zinged to the commander, who had kicked up his feet to rest atop the big desk. Stocking feet. With Mickey Mouse images dancing on them. Sidetracked, Mason struggled to pull his attention back to Mountain. "Meaning?"

"He's disappeared." Mountain let out a harsh breath, as if just saying that out loud, and maybe to the right people, could allow him to relax—at least a little.

The commander spoke up. "We need your help, Mason. You're uniquely qualified for this problem."

It didn't sound like he was qualified in any way for anything he'd heard so far. "Clarify." His spoken word was simplicity itself, but the tone behind it said he wanted the cards on the table ... now.

Mountain spoke up. "He's the third incident."

Mason's gaze narrowed, as the reports from the training

camp rolled through his mind. "One was Russian. One was from the German SEAL team. Both were deemed accidental deaths."

"No, they weren't."

There it was. The root of the problem in black-and-white. He studied Mountain, aiming for neutrality. "Do you have evidence?"

"My brother did."

"Ah, hell."

Mountain gave a clipped nod. "I'm going to find him."

"Of that I have no doubt," Mason said quietly. "Do you have a copy of the evidence he collected?"

"I have some of it." Mountain held out a USB key. "This is your copy. Top secret."

"We don't have to remind you, Mason, that lives are at stake," Doran added. "Nor do we need another international incident. Consider also that a group of scientists, studying global warming, is close by, and not too far away is a village home to a few hardy locals."

Mason accepted the key, turned to the commander, and asked, "Do we know if this is internal or enemy warfare?"

"We don't know at this point," Alpha replied through the phone. "Mountain will lead Shadow Recon. His mission is twofold. One, find out what's behind these so-called accidents and put a stop to it by any means necessary. Two, locate his brother, hopefully alive."

"And where do I come in?" Mason asked.

"We want you to pull together a special team. The members of Shadow Recon will report to both you and Mountain, just in case."

That was clear enough.

"You'll stay stateside but in constant communication with Mountain—with the caveat that, if necessary, you're on the next flight out."

"What about bringing in other members from the Mavericks?" Mason suggested.

Alpha took this question too, his response coming through via Speakerphone. "We don't have the numbers. The budget for our division has been cut. So we called the commander to pull some strings."

That was Doran's cue to explain further. "Mountain has fought hard to get me on board with this plan, and I'm here now. The navy has a special budget for Shadow Recon and will take care of Mountain and you, Mason, and the team you provide."

"Skills needed?"

"Everything," Mountain said, his voice harsh. "But the biggest is these men need to operate in the shadows, mostly alone, without a team beside them. Too many new arrivals will alert the enemy. If we make any changes to the training program, it will raise alarms. We'll move the men in one or two at a time on the same rotation that the trainees are running right now."

"And when we get to the bottom of this?" Mason looked from the commander back to Mountain.

"Then the training can resume as usual," Doran stated.

Mason immediately churned through the names already popping up in his mind. How much could he tell his men? Obviously not much. Hell, he didn't know much himself. How much time did he have? "Timeline?"

The commander's final word told him of the urgency.

"Yesterday."

Find Magnus here!

To find out more visit Dale Mayer's website.

smarturl.it/DMSSRMagnus

Author's Note

Thank you for reading Gage's Goal: Terkel's Team, Book 3! If you enjoyed the book, please take a moment and leave a short review.

Dear reader,

I love to hear from readers, and you can contact me at my website: www.dalemayer.com or at my Facebook author page. To be informed of new releases and special offers, sign up for my newsletter or follow me on BookBub. And if you are interested in joining Dale Mayer's Reader Group, here is the Facebook sign up page.
https://smarturl.it/DaleMayerFBGroup

Cheers,
Dale Mayer

Get THREE Free Books Now!

Have you met the SEALS of Honor?

SEALs of Honor Books 1, 2, and 3. Follow the stories of brave, badass warriors who serve their country with honor and love their women to the limits of life and death.

Read Mason, Hawk, and Dane right now for FREE.

Go here and tell me where to send them!
http://smarturl.it/EthanBofB

About the Author

Dale Mayer is a *USA Today* best-selling author, best known for her SEALs military romances, her Psychic Visions series, and her Lovely Lethal Garden cozy series. Her contemporary romances are raw and full of passion and emotion (Broken But ... Mending series). Her thrillers will keep you guessing (By Death series), and her romantic comedies will keep you giggling (*It's a Dog's Life*, a stand-alone novella; and the Broken Protocols series, starring Charming Marvin, the cat).

Dale honors the stories that come to her—and some of them are crazy and break all the rules and cross multiple genres!

To go with her fiction, she also writes nonfiction in many different fields, with books available on résumé writing, companion gardening, and the US mortgage system. She has recently published her Career Essentials series. All her books are available in print and ebook format.

Connect with Dale Mayer Online

Dale's Website – www.dalemayer.com
Twitter – @DaleMayer
Facebook – facebook.com/DaleMayer.author
BookBub – bookbub.com/authors/dale-mayer

Also by Dale Mayer

Published Adult Books:

Bullard's Battle
Ryland's Reach, Book 1
Cain's Cross, Book 2
Eton's Escape, Book 3
Garret's Gambit, Book 4
Kano's Keep, Book 5
Fallon's Flaw, Book 6
Quinn's Quest, Book 7
Bullard's Beauty, Book 8
Bullard's Best, Book 9

Terkel's Team
Damon's Deal, Book 1
Wade's War, Book 2
Gage's Goal, Book 3
Calum's Contact, Book 4

Kate Morgan
Simon Says... Hide, Book 1
Simon Says... Jump, Book 2
Simon Says... Ride, Book 3
Simon Says... Scream, Book 4

Hathaway House

Aaron, Book 1
Brock, Book 2
Cole, Book 3
Denton, Book 4
Elliot, Book 5
Finn, Book 6
Gregory, Book 7
Heath, Book 8
Iain, Book 9
Jaden, Book 10
Keith, Book 11
Lance, Book 12
Melissa, Book 13
Nash, Book 14
Owen, Book 15
Percy, Book 16
Hathaway House, Books 1–3
Hathaway House, Books 4–6
Hathaway House, Books 7–9

The K9 Files

Ethan, Book 1
Pierce, Book 2
Zane, Book 3
Blaze, Book 4
Lucas, Book 5
Parker, Book 6
Carter, Book 7
Weston, Book 8
Greyson, Book 9
Rowan, Book 10

Lovely Lethal Gardens

Lovely Lethal Gardens, Books 5–6
Lovely Lethal Gardens, Books 7–8
Lovely Lethal Gardens, Books 9–10

Psychic Vision Series
Tuesday's Child
Hide 'n Go Seek
Maddy's Floor
Garden of Sorrow
Knock Knock…
Rare Find
Eyes to the Soul
Now You See Her
Shattered
Into the Abyss
Seeds of Malice
Eye of the Falcon
Itsy-Bitsy Spider
Unmasked
Deep Beneath
From the Ashes
Stroke of Death
Ice Maiden
Snap, Crackle…
What If…
Talking Bones
Psychic Visions Books 1–3
Psychic Visions Books 4–6
Psychic Visions Books 7–9

By Death Series
Touched by Death

Haunted by Death
Chilled by Death
By Death Books 1–3

Broken Protocols – Romantic Comedy Series
Cat's Meow
Cat's Pajamas
Cat's Cradle
Cat's Claus
Broken Protocols 1-4

Broken and... Mending
Skin
Scars
Scales (of Justice)
Broken but... Mending 1-3

Glory
Genesis
Tori
Celeste
Glory Trilogy

Biker Blues
Morgan: Biker Blues, Volume 1
Cash: Biker Blues, Volume 2

SEALs of Honor
Mason: SEALs of Honor, Book 1
Hawk: SEALs of Honor, Book 2
Dane: SEALs of Honor, Book 3
Swede: SEALs of Honor, Book 4
Shadow: SEALs of Honor, Book 5

Heroes for Hire

Killian, Book 15
Hatch, Book 16
Corbin, Book 17
The Mavericks, Books 1–2
The Mavericks, Books 3–4
The Mavericks, Books 5–6
The Mavericks, Books 7–8
The Mavericks, Books 9–10
The Mavericks, Books 11–12

Collections
Dare to Be You…
Dare to Love…
Dare to be Strong…
RomanceX3

Standalone Novellas
It's a Dog's Life
Riana's Revenge
Second Chances

Published Young Adult Books:

Family Blood Ties Series
Vampire in Denial
Vampire in Distress
Vampire in Design
Vampire in Deceit
Vampire in Defiance
Vampire in Conflict
Vampire in Chaos
Vampire in Crisis

Vampire in Control
Vampire in Charge
Family Blood Ties Set 1–3
Family Blood Ties Set 1–5
Family Blood Ties Set 4–6
Family Blood Ties Set 7–9
Sian's Solution, A Family Blood Ties Series Prequel
    Novelette

Design series
Dangerous Designs
Deadly Designs
Darkest Designs
Design Series Trilogy

Standalone
In Cassie's Corner
Gem Stone (a Gemma Stone Mystery)
Time Thieves

Published Non-Fiction Books:

Career Essentials
Career Essentials: The Résumé
Career Essentials: The Cover Letter
Career Essentials: The Interview
Career Essentials: 3 in 1

Made in United States
North Haven, CT
24 May 2022

19470611R00134